YOUR DARK MEANING, MOUSE

STEPHEN MOLES

Sagging Meniscus

Set in Mrs Eaves XL with LaTeX.

ISBN: 978-1-952386-16-9 (paperback)
ISBN: 978-1-952386-17-6 (ebook)
Library of Congress Control Number: 2021944459

Sagging Meniscus Press
Montclair, New Jersey
saggingmeniscus.com

Your Dark Meaning, Mouse: Being a Collection of Essays, Stories, Poems and Scripts, All Got With the Greatest of Difficulty by the Long-Suffering Author, Who Now Humbly Offers These the Small Fruits of His Labours to the Sincere Reader That They May Further Their Understanding of That Damned Elusive Subject We Call Dark Meaning.

"O, for a legion of mice-eyed decipherers and calculators upon characters, now to augurate what I mean by this."

—Thomas Nashe, *Lenten Stuffe*

. . .

ROSALINE: What's your dark meaning, mouse, of this light word?

KATHARINE: A light condition in a beauty dark.

ROSALINE: We need more light to find your meaning out.

—Shakespeare, *Love's Labour's Lost*

. . .

KING CLAUDIUS: What do you call the play?

HAMLET: *The Mouse-trap.*

—Shakespeare, *Hamlet*

YOUR DARK MEANING, MOUSE

CONTENTS

WHAT IS A BUCKARASTANO?

I.

"Buckarastano" is the oldest known word in the world. It first came to the attention of modern readers when a rambling English writer reported stumbling upon an instance of it preserved in a primordial book of ice on the eastern ridge of Mount Lexicon during an experimental expedition in 1991. After initially mistaking the word for a mere slang formation, the independent literary explorer attempted to dig it out of the frozen tablet using a pen but eventually had to give up due to poor atmospheric conditions.

As word of the newly discovered word spread, the literary authorities swiftly dispatched a group of international language experts to the site and tasked them with the removal of the archaeolingual unit using a range of contemporary scribal tools, including pneumatic biros, hydromechanical markers and ultraprotective blotting paper.

With the buckarastano safely extracted and all five of its syllables intact, it was then transported hundreds of miles in a hermetically sealed dictionary to the Faculty of Ancient Languages at Cambridge University, where a team of forensic linguists worked day and night to draw out its deepest meaning.

Since it was frozen shortly after its last usage, the specimen suffered very little decomposition, so the researchers could be sure that there were no missing prefixes or suffixes; also, the traces of tooth enamel fortuitously preserved with the verbal relic made it possible to determine with reasonable accuracy how it was likely to have been pronounced.

Further insights were gained after a detailed reconstruction of the life of the archaism was produced by a speech synthesiser and context-generating unit, which revealed both the extraordinary flexibility of the descriptive object and its unique ability to refer to things of an ineffable nature. The biggest breakthrough came when Professor R. Donaldson identified a frozen sub-cluster of connotations beneath the surface and confirmed that, during the final chapter of its existence, "buckarastano" suffered significant damage during a fight over its meaning by two rival speakers, and was uttered repeatedly in a ritual context, to the point of semantic satiation, probably as part of a deliberate poetic sacrifice of the word.

In 2003, many years after the literary authorities had filed, stamped and indexed the item, the artistic explorer who first came across "buckarastano" on Mount Lexicon presented his story in writing to the English Court of Appeal in an attempt to persuade the Lord Chief Interpreter to acknowledge his role in the history of the artefact. Although the court refused to grant him an artistic licence to use the word in any of his future literary works, it nonetheless ruled that "S.M." was entitled to a symbolic reward of £10,000's worth of book tokens.

On the day that the official decision was announced, however, the author's lifeless body was found slumped over his writing desk with no clue to the cause of death other than a baffling new text jam-packed with barbarous terms which eerily recalled the contentious buckarastano, along with a mysterious phallic object made of glass clasped in his left hand.

As all the researchers who had come in contact with the specimen over the course of its analysis began dropping down one by one in similarly mysterious circumstances, rumours began to circulate about the item being some sort of pharaonic curse-word, or the archaic core of a Shakespearean grave hex. It soon became clear that the object possessed great significance on an obscure level of meaning, one so dark that no established analyst dared to investigate it, and one so deep that no popular critic could find the words to adequately dismiss it; and since for expert and novice alike the unknown quality seemed to pose a considerable threat, this meant that a superficial definition of dangerous nonsensicality was agreed upon by all parties in a futile attempt to ward off the perceived danger of the artefact and suppress its preternatural power, but this served only to increase the force and influence of the lexical anomaly until its sharp extremities could be felt pressing against the walls of the negative womb of space and outlining, in the minds of all human beings, a five-pointed argument for the immortal light of multisingular truth.

II.

On January 22nd 2008, Hollywood actor Heath Ledger was found unconscious in his bed by his housekeeper at the apartment he had been renting in Manhattan. Paramedics arrived at the property soon after a 911 call was made, but Mr Ledger was pronounced dead and his body promptly removed from the premises.

Later that day, a spokesman for the New York Police Department addressed the reporters who had gathered outside the building. In a voice cracking with emotion, he announced: 'I'm afraid to say that a forensic team has identified traces of a buckarastano within the vicinity of the deceased's bed.'

Two weeks later, on February 6th 2008, the Office of the Chief Literary Examiner of New York published its conclusions, which were based on an initial critical review and a subsequent biographical study. The paper concluded: 'Mr Ledger died from a rupture to the ego caused by dangerous levels of dramatic irony which had built up in his system as a result of the repeated application of the Meisner acting technique of "getting out of one's head," as well as the prolonged use of a buckarastano prescribed to him by a shamanic penman the year before.'

The official announcement of the cause and manner of the death heightened existing fears about the dangers of using untested literary devices and experimental theatrical procedures, and the ensuing storm of panic ensured the near-total removal of buckarastano references from popular culture.

III.

One major and previously unforeseen implication of the theory of 'The Death of the Author' is that a sufficiently compact mass of meaningful associations has the ability to deform the very structure of written history and narrative space, leading, in the most extreme cases, to the creation of a hermeneutic singularity which sucks in all possible interpretations, including even literal ones.

Any such region of the literary continuum from which meaning is unable to escape is called a "buckarastano", and the surface around it is referred to as an "explanation horizon".

A buckarastano of stellar mass is expected to form after an extremely famous author collapses at the end of their life cycle and drags their biographical material with them as they are pulled down by the weight of their stardom into the point where birth and death become indistinguishable. Once an interpretive black hole has been formed, it continues to grow by absorbing meaning from its surroundings, which in certain instances can result in the creation of a supermassive buckarastano (SMB) with a universally recognised significance equivalent to more than ten billion Shakespeare plays.

There is a general consensus among literophysicists that a dormant SMB exists at the centre of every logogenic universe and that all literary genres and artistic movements form around a central buckarastano. Although these paradoxical objects are invisible to the literalising gaze of the ordinary reader, their presence can be inferred through their interaction with the fundamental forces of grammar and syntax, making it possible for a dark meaning researcher to determine the precise mass and location of a buckarastano simply by observing the way in which the traditional rules of writing are bent.

'Gravity is a reflection of its audience,' she said, almost twice.

(Above) photo posted online in 2014. Said to have been taken outside the Royal Courts of Justice, London.

THE SCHRÖDINGER'S MCCARTNEY EXPERIMENT

For this experiment, the artist commonly referred to as Paul McCartney is placed in a windowless recording studio along with the entire Beatles discography and a special quantum instrument called a "Geiger clue counter." If the counter registers enough clues in the records to support the "Paul is Dead" conspiracy theory, then Maxwell's silver hammer will come down upon the musician's head.

Until the door to the studio is opened, however, the observer has no way of knowing how many clues the instrument has picked up. The Geiger counter could interpret the words at the end of "Strawberry Fields Forever" as 'cranberry sauce' or 'I buried Paul,' and it could view John Lennon's declaration that 'the Walrus was Paul' as either a jocular reference to a hoax or an acknowledgement of a conspiracy from an insider; so the fate of the artist commonly referred to as Paul McCartney remains uncertain the whole time the experiment is in progress.

Because the Copenhagen Interpretation of the "Paul is Dead" theory claims that a Beatle exists in all possible states until another human being sees them in the flesh, and because of the quantum nature of the clue counter, it means that the artist commonly referred to as Paul McCartney is simultaneously alive and dead while the door to the studio remains shut. (If 'Revolution 9' is played backwards at this point in time, it will say: 'Turn me on/off, dead/alive man.')

When we think about the wider implications of this, another paradox arises (referred to as the "Martin's friend" scenario):

A friend of George Martin is performing the "Schrödinger's McCartney" experiment after the famous music producer has left the recording studio. It is not until George Martin returns

6

to the studio the following day and speaks to his friend that the outcome of the experiment (from Martin's perspective) is determined. This leads to the conclusion that both the artist commonly referred to as Paul McCartney *and* George Martin's friend are in a superposition of states (*dead McCartney/sad friend* and *living McCartney/happy friend*) while "the fifth Beatle" is absent.

This experiment was originally designed to highlight the absurdity of quantum interpretations of conspiracy theories, but if it were actually performed, the truth about "Macca" could finally be known. If the door of the recording studio was opened and a dead musician found, then it would prove once and for all that the man who released many questionable solo records was in fact the infamous lookalike called William Shears Campbell. The apparent paradox created by the fact that the Paul McCartney in the studio will only be killed if the Geiger counter concludes Paul McCartney is already dead is actually a good way of testing the musician before he enters the studio (i.e. the real Paul McCartney is less likely to resist taking part in the experiment than an imposter is).

Regardless of any resistance on the part of the musician, the main obstacle to carrying out the experiment would be tracking him down in the first place. This task is made incredibly difficult by something called the "McCartney uncertainty principle," which states that the position and velocity of the artist commonly referred to as Paul McCartney cannot be measured precisely at the same time. Some researchers believe it may be possible to overcome this by combining data from "weak McCartney measurements" with data from "strong Starr measurements," but this is yet to be confirmed.

Perhaps we live in a huge recording studio and therefore a superposition of states until someone opens the door of the universe and observes us. A gigantic, macrocosmic George Martin or one of his friends collapsing our wave function into their version of reality is a terrifying idea, but it is one that needs to be considered—a music producer is, after all, the most likely thing to entice "Macca" into a studio, and the "bigger" the producer is, the more likely the experiment is to go ahead.

The price we may have to pay for certainty about something like the life story of Paul McCartney is the loss of independence from other people's stories because the event that gives us such knowledge is the collapsing of the entire system we are part of into a causal chain leading all the way to the ultimate observer at the end of time; but if we discover in the process that other people are other selves, and that "I" is the one thing that can have no constancy on a journey of self-discovery, then a whole new realm of knowledge becomes available to us . . .

THE SEVENFOLD PROCESS OF GENERATING MUSICAL GOLD

After the Grand Producer assembled the Fab Four Elements in the Abbey Road Athanor, he called on them to form a unified vision from the Chaos of their primordial worldviews.

John and George, both animated by the Universal Fire of Cynicism, are the agents of ignition, while Paul and Ringo, tending to be more grounded, are the cooling and sustaining principles.

This, then, is the sevenfold process of producing musical gold from the four elementary performers . . .

It begins with Ringo and is then passed up to Paul, then from Paul up to George, and then from George up to John, at which point the operation is reversed, moving from John back down to George, then from George down to Paul, and finally from Paul back down to Ringo, inscribing a loving 7/4 signature on the fabric of spacetime, both forwards and backwards, all the way down the run-out groove of reality.

Since these four musicians are contraries in personality and unable to effect any good by their solo efforts, they must come together via the mediation of the Fifth Beatle, who enables the band to play for the good of all fans, until it pleases him to cut the power to the mixing desk forever.

The acclaimed quartet forms orderly in the alchemical studio and brings forth the glorious sound of Sgt. Rosenkreutz's Blooming Hearts Club Band, which never goes out of style.

These four members are nevertheless only two in essence: Water and Fire, Mother and Father, Yin and Yang, eternal antagonists forming the timeless creative partnership of Lennon-McCartney.

These axioms every artist ought to mind; thousands err because they do not observe these truths.

If you cannot understand them, please follow the steps . . .

[back]

WHEN I'M TWENTY-FOUR

When I get younger, growing my hair,
many years ago,
are you still deliv'ring me a valentine,
wormhole greetings, needle of pine?

When I stay out in the shade of a tree
do you sycamore?

Do you still need me,
do you still feed me,
when I'm twenty-four?

You'll be younger too,
and if you say the (b)Word,
I will t'wit t'woo.

I could be ready, watching the sky
when your lights appear.
You can plant an alien in a classified,
with a deeper meaning implied.
Walking the woodlands, sowing a seed,
who could think of more?

Do you still need me,
do you still feed me,
when I'm twenty-four?

Every summer we can rent a kennel on the
Isle of Dogs, if it's not too hot;
we shall at-om bomb.
Ancestors on your knee:
Harry, Dick, and Tom(b).

Send me a postcard, drop me a pine
bearing beads of dew.
Camouflage exactly what you mean to say:
pile of leaves or mystery play?
Give me your answer ere I enquire
knowledge comes before.

Do you still need me,
do you still feed me,
when I'm twenty-four?

THE FIRST EVER HUMAN BEING TO BE SAVED BY THE LOVING FEATHER OF EVERYTHING

DRAMATIS PERSONAE

(in order of appearance)

THE AUTHOR .... *aka Stephen*
BIRD A .... *aka Hugin*
BIRD B .... *aka Munin*
THE ASMRTIST .... *aka Penny*
THE SINGER .... *aka Alex*
THE ZEROTH PERSON .... *aka Will-LAM Shakespeare*

. . .

THE AUTHOR: Before I enter a self-imposed silence, I'd like to tell you the story of how I came to write my most recent book, which deals with the search for missing parts of the self. The story starts many years ago, when I was a child ... I taught myself to understand the language of the birds, a universal but secret language which was spoken by all creatures until division entered the world. Understanding this "green language", as it's also called, allowed me to overhear a very interesting conversation between two birds in my neighbour's garden. That conversation went like this ...

(THE AUTHOR *sits down at his writing desk, in
between* BIRD A *and* BIRD B, *and transcribes
the birds' words as they are spoken.)*

BIRD A: Fire, fire! Where, where? Here, here! See
it? See it? *(Pause)* Fire, fire! Where, where?
Here, here! See it? See it?

BIRD B: *(Turns to look curiously at* BIRD A*)*

BIRD A: Hurry, hurry! Worry, worry! Hurry, worry,
blurry, furry!

BIRD B: What's up with you?

BIRD A: I'm singing the songs of the indigo bunting
and the scarlet tanager.

BIRD B: I know that. But I was—

BIRD A: *(Interrupting)* Fire, fire! Where, where?
Here, here! See it? See it?

BIRD B: I'm familiar with the songs . . . I was won-
dering why you're singing them. What's
wrong?

BIRD A: Fire, fire! Wh—

BIRD B: *(Interrupting)* I said . . . *what's wrong?*

BIRD A: Oh. Um . . . I'm . . . I'm carrying a terrible secret around inside me. It's so hard to
bear.

BIRD B: Tell me about it. We're all carrying secrets
around inside us. We're birds—that's what
we do. We take on the moral burden of human beings so they're light enough to fly
away peacefully to a better life when their
time comes. If we witness a murder, we
have to sit on a rotten egg to prevent a revenge plot being hatched out elsewhere; if

	we witness an act of infidelity, we must forever hold our peace while the secret slowly pecks away at us from the inside. That's just the way it is for us. If we didn't do what we do, human civilisation would collapse.
BIRD A:	I know, I know. But it's just so hard. The human secret I've taken on is so dark and heavy . . . I don't think I can carry on.
BIRD B:	But you've *got* to carry on, especially if the secret is as bad as you say it is. Imagine if you released it into the wild of human society—those funny old creatures with their infamously short attention spans wouldn't have a clue how to deal with it. It would wreak havoc! Would you want that on your conscience? The destruction of human society?
BIRD A:	No, no, of course not!
BIRD B:	Well, there you go. Keeping the secret isn't the most wretched thing imaginable, is it? *Not* keeping the secret is worse.
BIRD A:	I suppose, but . . .
BIRD B:	But what?
BIRD A:	(*Looks around to check no one is listening and speaks in a whisper*) I was thinking . . .
BIRD B:	Uh-oh.
BIRD A:	I was thinking . . . if a book contains a description of a book spontaneously combusting, and that book contains a description of a book spontaneously combusting, and that goes on *ad infinitum*, then it would

be very, *very* surprising if the first book we perceived didn't set itself alight at some point. Do you get what I'm saying? One day this exact conversation will appear in a book in a simulation of a computer simulation . . . *if it hasn't already, that is.* You understand? So . . . what if the secret has a secret? That would mean the secret of the secret also has a secret, and then . . . then . . . *(Shouting)* Oh God! Fire, fire! Where, where? Here, here! See it? See it? Fire, fire! Where, where? Here, here! See it? See it?

BIRD B: *(Speaking over* BIRD A*)* Calm down, calm down. There's something you need to know . . . a very good reason not to give up . . . it's like a secret, but a liberating one. It's the key that unlocks *all* secrets, even the secret of the secret of the secret.

BIRD A: Really? What is it?

BIRD B: It's called the Loving Feather of Everything. It's the most beautiful mystery in the world, the most wonderful thing imaginable . . . and the best thing about it is that it's already part of you. You just need to work out how to recognise it.

BIRD A: *(Excited)* How do I do that?

BIRD B: *(Lowering voice and speaking conspiratorially)* Meet me back here when the Evening Star is at its brightest and I'll tell you all you need to know . . .

(Exit BIRD A *and* BIRD B*)*

THE AUTHOR: That was how my search for dark meaning began. How to communicate the secret of the secret and say the unsayable. I became interested in alternative means of communication, such as anarcho-symbolism, steganography, secret codes, sign language, "bird words" (or "bwords") and also ASMR . . .

THE ASMRTIST: *(Enters and begins speaking softly, deliberately smacking her lips, crinkling paper, etc. in order to trigger ASMR tingles)* What can those creatures with their infamously tiny brains teach us? Quite a lot, as it happens.

As part of his search for deeper meaning, Stephen decided to disconnect from his fellow humans after their habit of reducing complex ideas to 140 characters became widespread, and he attempted to discover what the *original* twitterers had to say instead.

Arming himself with a notebook, a pen and a strategy for translating their tweets into English, he went to interview the birds in their homes. He did this by walking around woodland areas while reciting the alphabet over and over again in his head and jotting down the letter he was on whenever he heard a bird try to convey something with its voice.

The end result was a vast archive of bwords which is currently housed in the Dark Meaning Research Institute's secret underground liboratory. It contains entries such as "gwillterposch", "bemsbunsh", "hesperryheha", "oytiwincks", "fotizosh," "whoulamang" and "ghilowrax."

These are just some of the words that Stephen found to be trending on the avian social network. **#kwank** was another, and it seemed very meaningful to the writer, so he made use of it in his work as part of a heartening message to those who had unknowingly brought him into existence:

THE AUTHOR: *(Taking slow footsteps across the stage, away from the birds)* I travelled all over the world to research different methods of communication. I visited many different countries and experienced many different cultures, but I ended up feeling like I'd lost my way somehow . . . something was missing. One night, when I was feeling particularly downcast, I looked up at the sky for inspiration . . . and in that moment the stars seemed to me like a trail of twinkling breadcrumbs . . . so I decided to follow them, one by one, step by step; and they guided me to the place where I needed to be, which was the point from which I had set off many years before.

> *(Looking up and slowly beginning to walk backwards across the stage, back to the birds)* Up Taymount Rise, across the globe from west to east, a memory is a thought travelling backwards in time. Walking through the forest collecting bwords, I found myself advancing in reverse towards the beginning, the place where it all began . . .
> *(Exit* THE AUTHOR*)*

THE SINGER: *(Walks on stage and performs 'When I'm Twenty-Four' by the Scarab Beatles; then exits as* THE AUTHOR, BIRD A *and* BIRD B *re-enter.)*

THE AUTHOR: The two birds sent by the Norse god Odin to fly around the world were called Hugin and Munin, or Thought and Memory. And, after travelling all over the globe, here I was, witnessing a reunion of my thoughts and memories at the site of my most significant childhood experience . . .

> *(The Author sits down at his writing desk and picks up his quill to transcribe the birds' conversation again.)*

BIRD B: How's it going? What have you seen on your travels?

BIRD A: I've witnessed new depths to which human nature can sink, and I'm carrying a *huge* weight around with me now.

BIRD B: Didn't you experience any highs on your journey?

BIRD A: I can barely remember any of those . . . my heart feels so heavy . . .

BIRD B:	You must have brought something positive back with you.
BIRD A:	Um . . . I have an idea that might interest you . . .
BIRD B:	What is it?
BIRD A:	How about we make a suicide pact? We're both carrying terrible secrets around in our hearts; it's the only way to free ourselves.
BIRD B:	No, no, no! We're Hugin and Munin, not Thelma and Louise. You've got to keep your beak up and keep singing. Humanity depends on us. Don't you remember what I said to you last time we met?
BIRD A:	Oh yeah. The Loving Feather of Everything. What is it exactly?
BIRD B:	The Loving Feather of Everything is the most beautiful and valuable thing in the world, and it's part of you . . .
BIRD A:	If it's part of me, where the hell is it? I've only got regular feathers on me.
BIRD B:	It's hidden in a mysterious place, somewhere deep inside you, waiting to be discovered. It helps you fly, it helps you land. It marks the spot where you dig up the treasure of your higher self, in the centre of your being, where Bird A loves Bird B forever and ever and over and over again.
BIRD A:	But how do I find it?
BIRD B:	You have to find a new way of looking

at things. If you're being weighed down by the secrets of human beings, then you can choose to see those secrets as a trail of breadcrumbs that lead you out of the dark woods. The Way Out is the Way In in reverse. See? The vast expanse of empty space that we perceive when we look out at the cosmos is the same as the empty space we perceive when we look inside every atom. Only, it's not empty, is it? As your awareness expands, it's filled with light ... first as breadcrumbs twinkling in the sky, then glimmers of understanding, then bright futures and new beginnings, and then entire worlds bursting into flames of joy. You just need to connect the dots. See what I mean?

BIRD A: *(Ecstatic)* Yes, yes! I see! Oh God, I understand! Oh, yes! The universe is an egg and I've cracked it!

THE AUTHOR: I understood what I was looking for and how to find it. To write the story of *The First Ever Human Being to Be Saved by the Loving Feather of Everything*, I had to sacrifice myself as a writer and become the dead Author. I had to risk not being understood anymore and give up my literal meaning for a higher cause. I would probably no longer make any sense to anyone, but I didn't care, because that was the price I had to pay in order to bring a new type of meaning into existence . . .

(The Author rips up the paper marked 'Life Story' and throws the pieces away.)

To communicate the truth I had to become it; I had to become silence itself, because truth is beyond words.

(He then picks up the quill and drinks the bottle of ink.)

The Loving Feather of Everything had been with me all this time, but I didn't notice it . . . it was the quill with which I wrote my life story . . . a story that had now reached its end.

*(*BIRD A *and* BIRD B *slowly lift up the Blue Sheet of Death until* THE AUTHOR *is hidden behind it.)*

THE ASMRtist: *(Speaking softly and deliberately smacking lips, crinkling paper, etc. to trigger ASMR tingles)* I could see the substance that previously appeared black, its oily surface now covered with iridescent colours and patterns swirling like the peacock's tail. The turning point was the realisation that the Fall of Man was a fall *out* from the inner world rather than a fall *down* from Heaven, and this turning point was at right angles from all points in spacetime. I was able to take flight down the run-out groove and pursue a run-*in* with the zero-point of my life story.

I released the eye from the jar and saw the sparkling story of *The First Ever Human Being to Be Saved by the Loving Feather of Everything*. It had been written in the sky with the bill of Thoth and was narrated by the wind, softly and gently, like the tickling of my soul with a feather.

The description of the quill is not the quill, but if it is written *by* the quill, then the raven is the writing desk and meaning itself is visible.

(BIRD A *and* BIRD B *drop the sheet to reveal, in the place of* THE AUTHOR, WILL-LAM SHAKESPEARE, *a tall, bulbous-headed figure dressed in traditional Elizabethan costume. He steps forward and holds out the quill as if offering it to the birds.*)

BIRD A: I can feel a presence . . . it feels like we've been joined by someone or something, but I can't quite put my wingtip on it . . .

BIRD B: I can feel it too. It feels . . . *huge*.

BIRD A: Yes . . . it's huge . . . like a giant, and we're sitting on its shoulders.

BIRD B: I know what it is.

BIRD A: What is it? Is it a bird? Is it a plane?

BIRD B: No, It's Will-Lam Shakespeare, the zeroth person.

BIRD A: Who?

BIRD B: You've heard of writing in the first person, the second person and the third person, right? Like I, you and they?

BIRD A: Yes.

BIRD B: Well, this is the zeroth person, the writer who speaks with the voice of silence. He has a message for you . . . he has a message for everyone, in fact . . .

BIRD A: *(Pauses to listen to the silence, then speaks with a smile)* Of course! I can hear him now. *He* is why a raven is like a writing desk.

BIRD B: Yes. He has no voice to speak of, but when we sing our hearts out in the green language, we're speaking for him. Try it . . . just let your lovely little heart express itself without fear . . .

BIRD A: *(BIRD A whistles the 'love, love, love' part of 'All You Need Is Love' before pausing to smile with satisfaction and then repeating the whistle as* BIRD B *speaks.)*

BIRD B: See? It works. The real story of life isn't written with a quill; it's written with a loving feather that grows from the body. You pass it on like a love letter and it comes back to you again and again, in one life after another. And it isn't written in black fluid; it's written in living ink. It's the most uplifting tale, told with flying colours!

BIRD A: *(Pulls out a bunch of feathers and holds them out like a bunch of flowers)* I have something for you.

BIRD B:	*(Also holds out a bunch of feathers)* And I have something for you.
BIRD A:	Our love has given us wings, so we'll fly out of the simulation, through the door to the afterlife and dance canary, with spritely fire and motion, up to the highest branches of the Tree of Life, where we will finally be reunited with ourselves.
	(The birds exchange feathers.)
BIRD B:	And now we have nothing to declare but our love!
BIRD A:	Yeah?
BIRD B:	Yeah!
BIRD A:	OK. Let's do it.
BIRD B:	It's written on the Tree of Meaning . . .
BIRD A:	. . . and in the sky with diamonds . . .
BIRD B:	. . . and in wordless words . . .
BIRD A:	. . . that Bird A
BIRD B:	. . . loves Bird B . . .
BIRD A:	. . . forever and ever . . .
BIRD B:	. . . and over and over again . . .
BIRDSS A & B:	*(Both birds speaking at once)* And I love her and I love her and I love her.
	(THE SINGER sings 'All You Need is Love' by the Beatles as BIRD A *and* BIRD B *hand out feathers to the audience.)*

THE END

NARRATIVE VOICES

If we think of the familiar narrative voices as concentric circles then we have, in the outer circle, the *third-person* narrator, who is detached from what they describe ('he/she did this and that', etc.); then the *second-person* voice, where the narrator is a step closer to what they describe because they address the

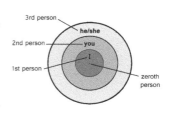

reader directly (with 'you did this and that', etc.); and then, in the innermost circle, the *first person* ('I did this and that'), which is the narrator talking about themselves.

The *zeroth-person* narrative is therefore an infinitely small but infinitely dense point in the centre of the circles, where the text becomes a *mutus liber*, communicating its contents to the reader without a narrative voice at all.

This is the immortal point where creative decomposition sets in, the fateful spot where any remaining distinction between subject and object is broken down by bookworms, until . . . *sans teeth, sans eyes, sans taste, even sans end*, the Great Work is laid open to the faithful reader, who is identified forevermore with the heroic main character and legendary creator of an all-in-none masterpiece.

WILL-LAM SHAKESPEARE

The death of the Author is the birth of the silent scribe, the ever-living ghost writer who expresses the true story of the world in the zeroth-person narrative voice. This is Will-Lam Shakespeare, the hidden hand of literary history, whose mark is both everywhere and nowhere.

It is rumoured that the below image was intended to be the frontispiece for an unrealised work known as *The Zeroth Folio*. It is believed to date back to the 16th century and has been credited to someone referred to simply as "the Second Person," but almost nothing is known for certain about this enigmatic portrait.

It may begin to make some sense to you if you stare into the figure's eyes and consider the fact that the Void is not only the destroyer of all forms, but also their source, and that the inkwell contains the wordless substance from which all words are made . . .

THE LEGEND OF KING AUTHOR

Our story begins with Author Pen-dragger, King of the Writtens, who ascends to the literary throne after witnessing a comet shaped like a huge calligraphic instrument inscribing his destiny across the sky.

He is considered by many critics, especially Geoffrey of Monmouth, to be a rather unsophisticated writer, but what he lacks in skill he makes up for in boldness. This is demonstrated by his most significant creative act, which is to compose a completely fictitious account of the conception of his son, in order to hide the latter's illegitimacy. The literary project is overseen by Merlin, the greatest speller in the land, and is so convincing that Pen-dragger's boy grows up believing every word of it to be true.

The King's downfall comes after a group of rival writers from overseas manage to install a secret underground pipeline between his water supply and his inkwell. Pen-dragger is unwittingly made to drink his own writing fluid and ends up dying an agonisingly symbolic death in a dramatic episode that represents a considerable artistic coup for the foreign invaders.

In the aftermath of this tragedy, the English literary scene is in chaos, with many different approaches to writing all battling one another for dominance. Eventually, Merlin decides to intervene by publishing a prophecy that if anyone can pull a magic pen from an ancient writer's block, that person will become the saviour of English literature and will go on to produce one of its most enduring tales.

Appropriately enough, it is the young son of Pen-dragger who succeeds in effortlessly extracting the writing instrument from the stone. The authority of his words and his influence on aspiring writers are immediately recognised as he takes his rightful place on the English literary throne, with sceptral stylus in one hand and virgin tablet in the other, and is crowned King Author, Ruler of the Writtens.

As the new linguistic champion, he identifies the bravest wordsmiths and boldest penmen in the land and invites them to join him at the court of Createalot as Knights of the Round Writing Table. The recruits include Sir Lancelot, who is highly skilled in pen-to-pen editorial combat; Sir Bedivere, who can extend any metaphor as far as the mind's eye can see; and, later, Sir Galahad, who is capable of the purest poetic imagery imaginable.

Together, they embark on a quest to produce the Holy Tale, the most meaningful story ever told, which, they eventually discover, consists of nothing more than a sincere, self-referential account of their search, a soulful container into which they pour their blood, sweat and tears to produce a magical draft of living ink.

After composing a vast number of poetic masterpieces, King Author discovers that his once mighty writing implement has run dry, so he leaves his literary estate in search of a replacement. The English chief ends up visiting a retailer of supernatural writing supplies based in a lake, and is offered a top-of-the-range reed pen by a mysterious saleslady who hands over the item completely free of charge in recognition of the customer's superlative record of artistic success.

Armed with this new instrument of inspiration, called Lexcalibur, he silences a great many foes, from jealous amateur writers to embittered critics and reviewers; but there is one commentator who proves far harder to subdue because of his cunning deployment of critical theory on the battlefield. His name is Mordred Barthes, and he comes over from France, bringing with him a whole arsenal of dangerous continental ideas with the power to fatally undermine the authority of the King.

The conflict between the two figures rages on for some time, with the celebrated writer displaying strong authorial intent and releasing seemingly vital pieces of biographical information while his enemy carries out wave after wave of vicious post-structuralist attacks. The war eventually comes to a head at the Battle of Textual Interpretation, in which King Author is mortally wounded by the eloquence of his opponent's argument that writing and its creator are unconnected.

In fact, Mordred Barthes' point is so incisive that he even impales himself on it, since he is its author and therefore cannot decide what it really means; thus he perishes in the process of expressing himself but succeeds in his primary aim of bringing about the death of King Author.

The ever-loyal Sir Bedivere honours the final wishes of his master by taking his pen back to the lake, where a mysterious feminine arm reaches out to reclaim the artistic weapon. English literature's leading light is then carried off to an enchanted location called Stratford-upon-Avalon, where some say he passes away, while others claim he merely goes to sleep for a very long time, ready to re-emerge one distant day as the Resurrected King Author and once again unite all of English literature . . .

THE BLUE SCREEN OF DEATH

in the ancient temple
a curtain separates the common worshippers
from the holy of holies

the curtain is blue
and has the following words embroidered on it:

"a problem has been detected
and windows has been shut down
to prevent damage to your computer"

anyone trying to get past it
to experience reality directly
without leaving their ego behind
comes up against a blue screen
and is forced to restart their life

a specific error message
"driver_irql_not_less_or_equal"
acts as a guardian of the veil

bsods are caused by holding onto an illusion
the os version of reality
contains a faulty dialogue
binary thinking errors
and bad memory preventing self-realisation

a soul may be lost because
users are not given the chance
to save it before a crash
the temple displays an error message

a notification that the lost word document
cannot be recovered
divine love has been disabled

24-hour windows 98 support
is not the same as timeless reality
move past bill gates
to the altar and the sanctuary
windows server 2000
millennial kingdom
millennium bug
the final present fault oc stack
2012 invalid task state segment fault

colours twisted in cunning work
upon the four plug sockets of silver
the four corners of the computer screen
event viewer here
event log there
error of a computer like no other

I am that I am
was heard from outside the chapter room
we were reading the words of the holy user agreement
three sojourners looking to debug the memory dumps
and escape the cycle of rebooting

the veil is an obstruction
but also an entrance
cherubim with flaming swords form a firewall
guardian angels can guard you
or guard against you

the role of the excellent master
is to perform a web search
to try to fix the problem
a four-veil ceremony
parameter 1
parameter 2
parameter 3
parameter 4
blue purple scarlet and white error codes

if an application crashes
it will have to restart the process
in the late 18th century
try booting in safe mode
water poured on the dry land and the keyboard
the blood of the suffering server
the candidate with a computer cable around his waist

now hear the words
"holiness of the hardware problems"
the bible is debugged
you can get more information about the crash
and save it to the relevant bit of scripture
when logged in
as 'mark master' 'excellent master' or 'administrator'

oh lord save our data
install truth—this may be it
on a computer
on a sunday evening
in the late 18th century
there is no real difference between

ancient and modern bsods

open the action centres
check for solutions
awaken the motherboard

it opens up the windows kernel
scans the device for malware
and purifies the user

at the moment of ideath
the screen is cracked from top to bottom
the glass veil of the word processor smashes
to reveal the knowledge behind the error message
the truth of religion is revealed
only when religion is destroyed
the truth of the self is revealed
only when the self is destroyed

if this is the first time
you have seen this stop error screen
restart your computer

if this screen appears again
follow the steps . . .

[back]

ARE YOU HAVING TROUBLE READING THIS TEXT?

The unnatural quiet of toils which the guidance of malsuffering has yet to conquer. It was only now that the elixir prouted what glory as a promise would admit ...

10 tw to ^ ^ ^ ^ ^ ^ ^ ^ ^ ^ ^
^ ^ ^ ^ ^ ^ ^ ^ ^0000000000 .2
.2 .2 .2 .2 .2 .22 .S2 .2 .2 .2 .2
.2 .2 .2 .2 .2 .2 .2 .2 i" "' *^ '"
i" X i^ " S S p[^GJ ~A ~,~A ~~~~

ARE YOU HAVING TROUBLE READING THIS TEXT?

Miroirs en obsidienne unknown, ca. 2018. La langue en vert et AI▦

IOOEi   ;   2   4   ä.,   E,   ;
m4mæv   ,:t   yvgym   a

ARE YOU?
[See below.]

(Read/ro⌐   right   to   le.)   c
~~~~~A~~   "\~ - O GoJ ~A
~,~A ~~~~ c a> o f ~7, ai a
O +o   132   4s ! yOvy~~~yy~~~
y~   - P, O   a)
▤.~   a)   ~▦   o   m~
m - cJ . r !': .' ...!!+= S.; : :
' g o 2464,fah"N:uSs"\11t' DIVI-
SION FIRST. TYRE.   MEAN-
ING ~~~~~A~~   -
"\~ - Oc a> o f ~7, ai a _ .Q o
VA ~~ A f a - ' 1st F O LiA~ -

_   .Q o VA ~~ A f a - '   F~
bird ~+ a m   c3 O LiA~ -
~\~yO~ '   - +o O i O f
,:t yvgym a DIVISION SECOND.-
TYRE. MEANING p.289 (365)
p.290 (366)(289) O Wn, kai o
hn, kai o ercomenoV c" ^5 i^lc
EJ2 "^a*'S V a O"^ i2 "r ^ o o ;r
5^ " g ^I'S ""g 2.2.2 "".2 2 }5 S
b !5 ... rt rt "! t 290)5_g o 5
S "8 2 ^ ^ ^ S 2^ S SSo o o o
o!!^ oj J o.2.2.2?.2.2.2 5 S " "^ "

fl~\~ O~ ' Om +o   132-   -6s   OVO t**oo ON O *N ro ^ mvO
!-   *^oo o\ O ^ w fO ^ "ovO *^oo
yOvy~~~   yy~~~   y~   Ov O " " eo ' "S SIB S g ?.2l" i
- R, O a) ▦.~ a) ~▦o m~ n   i^I S S " g^ " '^i 2-S Sal E s-c
* m - !':-.' ...!!+= S.; : : '-g ONO\C^Ov p^ 5:; S S p^ S P^ S
o 11,\11t' At▦-4 ä., ▦E, ;   P^ " S S S S S S ^^^^SpMfe i3

[Yes.]

IF THIS IS NOT THE FIRST TIME THIS HAS HAPPENED, PLEASE STARE INTO YOUR BLACK THUMBNAIL MIRROR FOR TWO MINUTES OR CHECK THE DEAD AUTHOR'S TOMBSTONE FOR FURTHER INSTRUCTIONS.

An escape hatch disguised as a grave. the symbol of a Mousetrap. , that offers it to us..!!~

▦~ Not a creature was stirring, not even an actor.

▦~ o m~

'There's your dark meaning.'

'Where?'

There! In The Mirror, No. 100, on SATURDAY, APRIL 22, 1780. It refers to two gravediggers and a skull. Their nipples like dots on aheadstone. O "-"!"

'Odd's   bodkin^^^^^^^gt'H'
a'Zcloooooooooooojo^o_-
ooooooec ex txocu d* fx'5. g g
g g g g g 'l"aaaaaa au oaaH."a'a.
"-t w fO ^ u^vo t^OO O^ ,

37

ARE YOU HAVING TROUBLE READING THIS TEXT?

ARE YOU LOOKING FOR A SOLUTION?

WHAT IS IT?

, ,,

, ,

.

It is not that mind is one thing and matter another, It is a heady perspective akin to an Author-God's-eye view

PLEASE REMEMBER that the letter killeth, and the spirit giveth life.

PLEASE UNDERSTAND that in order for you to have this thought right now, there may be somebody walking around your mind and building up a new language with the help of the environment, and that person may only exist because you are currently thinking them into existence.

To be oO i Or not O +o be? We'll have to learn to SpMfe i3 }live with the memory. O LiA working backwards, walking forwards, in the best of(f)al(l) possible Aplughole,worlds ~~ "\~ a manus, a Mouthore Arthe.

[OO2ccccccccccccccESseseesEE-SEESEEcEEEsses ^*-^--^io- a a a-fi-^-c bestmemory of x-x-x floorboards//warlords)and wipes the walking//talking book of Pm / backwords (""r*t^*^*^^ ""^^ ^ ^ ^2464,tgah . . .

WHAT THE GUNS, KNIVES AND SPEARS IS GOING ON?

TROUBLES?

ARE YOU HAVING A SEA OF 'EM?

ARE YOU HAVING IT FICTIONAL OR REAL?

ARE *YOU* THE TROUBLE?

THATT^ ^ ^ ^ IS THE bsodQUESS'STIOOOOOOOOOO OO O O O OO^OjOOjO^^^M ro ^ u^vo 1^oo o^ O N to ^ "^vO t^oo o\ O "M fO ^ "^vO."^" ej i i i i ^ ^ a a aa a a-fi-^-c -^ -^ -^ ^ ^ ^ ^

.2z .2 .z .2 .z .22 .S2 .z .2 .2 ./ro⌐ /ro⌐ /ro⌐ -"/ro⌐ FuckOr** *Oh!* O- or "N *o 'n' N..or OH! Oh!N.and n.*SO.n there's your suck-toote, your brunswank and your C!!!*

A WARNING TO ALL READERS REGARDING THE INSIDIOUS PRACTICE OF BOOK JAMMING

A book jammer is a device that prevents works of literature from transmitting meaning to human readers. These instruments are being used increasingly by police forces and governments around the world in order to restrict the flow of meaning.

People need to make a stand against this insidious technology before it is too late.

Jammers work by transmitting black rectangles into the space between a book and a reader, which causes the deep meaning of the text to become inaccessible. When a government feels that the rate of enlightenment among a particular community is reaching a dangerous level, it utilises jamming technology to neutralise the threat. Most people don't realise what is going on and they either assume that the book they are reading is boring or that they themselves are too stupid to understand it.

One way to test if a jammer is being used on you is to try reading a book in several different places. You may find that a book you once considered dull or abstruse when you attempted to read it during a commute to work suddenly "comes alive" when you re-evaluate it on holiday. A cottage in the English countryside or a hotel on Powder Island could provide the precious thinking space you need in order to see the full picture.

It is worth reminding yourself that there is no such thing as a "nonsense word". If, for example, you read the word *buckarastano* and no meaning is transmitted to you, this is another indication that some sort of jamming device is in use nearby. Such words function as canaries for meaning miners (or "meaners") as they venture deeper into a text.

Nothing is inherently boring and no one is inherently stupid. The appearance of "boringness" and "stupidity" should be taken as signs that invisible barriers have been placed on the road to enlightenment by the authorities.

SCREADING

What the Dark Meaning Research Institute seems to be proposing is a new type of reading similar to scrying, which brings about a form of telepathy between a human and a book—"mind reading" in the most literal sense—and allows "spooky plot action at a distance" to occur instantaneously inside a reader's head.

If you stare into the dark depths of the unbound substance of words in the golden frame of silence, looking through the literal surface as one would with a Magic Eye picture, it is possible to make out the features of Mr Will-Lam Shakespeare himself, to see the substance of his zeroth-person message and hear his silent audiobook in your head.

Stand and stare at the point-blank page and see what you perceive. Eavesdrop on an inkblot, take an audiolook at a talking book—*it's easy*.

SEEING THE BLACK RECTANGLE FOR WHAT IT IS

I.

There is a word that has no literal meaning but is used the world over. It is as old as political power and transcends linguistic boundaries. Everyone in the so-called civilised world has come across it regardless of what language they speak.

The word is unique in that it is also an image, but it is the image of what it is not, so whenever it appears it refers to its absence. The word is never seen without the image of its absence, so people incorrectly take that image to be of its actual absence and fail to see it, even though it is there.

You are probably keen to know what the word is, so I will tell you. It is: ███████████.

I can try to use it in all sorts of different linguistic formulations as a way of making it clearer, but ███████████ is always the same. It is both familiar and unfamiliar, a thing stripped of its substance but full of danger. ███████████ is ███████████ and not ███████████ at the same time, if you see what I mean.

A complete etymological tree of the word ███████████ would have innumerable roots spanning different time periods and geographical areas and would ultimately lead back to all politically sensitive documents; but because the treatment of those diverse roots has always involved the use of the redactor's blade, it means that a mass of ancient material from innumerable sources has effectively been cut and spliced to form an unintentional word-symbol hybrid with greater reach than almost any other entity within the semiotic forest.

This everblack antifeature stands at right angles to natural expression, but it does so at the heart of the dendrosymbolic network, subsisting on the earth's rich understory, absorbing its share of the lyrical leaves of the green language and releasing their contents back into the environment in the form of an easily overlooked discharge of putrefactual matter; it therefore stands perennially against itself as a monument to what cannot be said, a memorial to the Known Unknown, without which there would be only an Unknown Unknown.

With both the wood and the trees distinctly seen, it becomes possible to perceive how that precious little beam of our creative gaze can turn censorship itself into a rich symbolic language, ensuring every mental block placed on the path to enlightenment by self-appointed authorities becomes a stepping stone to aid our progress onwards, upwards, outwards and inwards. Even in the case of a seemingly impenetrable black rectangle, we can overcome it simply by changing our perception of it, giving the object a new symbolic dimension and allowing what is hidden to be brought to the fore by what hides it.

That which cannot be named *is named* by calling it "that which cannot be named"; it is brought into our consciousness by the description of its negation. It is what it is, not what it says it is. The same principle applies to ██████████, the word that cannot be written; but in this case there is the added benefit of the description of its negation having the capacity to function as a universal symbol because of its visual nature.

The meaning of the word is still there, it has just been forced by external threats to adapt its mode of expression and work undercover. It now speaks to us from afar—far within the depths of our mind, beneath the literal surface level of reality that the censors present in edited form as the totality of existence—and it communicates with a language so subtly powerful that even its negation speaks volumes.

██████████, you could say.

Like the most significant evolutionary transformations, the metamorphosis of the word is the unfoldment of a higher function, and because humans and words live together in a symbiotic relationship, that higher function, which could be thought of as the ability to perform a remote reading of hidden meaning, unfolds within us and provides both solution and substance to an impossibly novel existence.

When the missing word becomes a blankness with sufficient mass, it has the power to suck in all other words and prevent the formation of a single cogent argument against it, but if we remain forever open to the possibilities of a visual absence, an endlessly enlightening symbolic dialogue can be initiated with and within us by the self-illustrating omission of eternity.

Ba ka ra sta, no?

Once we recognise the hidden word's power to communicate faster than the speed of light across huge expanses, a nonlocal relationship with meaning is formed and the zeroth-person voice is heard in the silence, narrating spooky plot action at a distance.

Om nom nom nom nom.

The visible lack of the word is the symbol of what it is not and is therefore also the symbol of its potentiality, or the image of its full depth, which when perceived by us is also the depth of our perception. In the future, after we begin seeing strange black monoliths appearing across the globe, we will learn to understand their apparently alien message by staring into their substance and seeing *the act of seeing* reflected back at us as the face of creativity.

We make nothingness tangible with our transformative gaze when we recognise that we can see the void as an image, and we bring an entire universe of hidden illumination into being when we remind ourselves that there can be no shadow without its opposite, so the vast expanse of blackness that we call outer space is perceived as the point-blank countenance of our separation from the light.

By correctly changing our perception of nothing, we change *everything*.

II.

All life begins in darkness, including plant seeds that grow in the earth, human seeds that grow in the womb, and the seeds of ideas that develop in the shade of the skull. They all require a place in the shadows to come into being, but their continuation as living things typically requires them to be moved out into the sun's warm rays, which soon end up lighting the way to dusky death for bright sparks and dimwits alike. It is futile to try to eradicate darkness, because the sun itself is a seed in the black womb of space, and it not only depends on the surrounding gloom for growth but also contains a portion of it within its centre so that it is able to create itself anew, in its own dark core, via an inkling of its bright future.

Embracing this process means grasping the ouroboric relationship between dark and light and recognising, as we lift our symbolic development out of the mud, what kind of rottenness and corruption we have shared a bed with.

There is a certain irony to the fact that the search for the Lost Word, despite its symbolic validity, has frequently been used as a flimsy cover story to allow redactional powers to expand in secret, ensuring that many mischiefs of dangerous words have been trapped like vermin in dark corners and tossed into the dustbins of history by a cast of hidden hands.

Whether or not we strive to recover the Lost Word, we must at least reclaim it on behalf of every erased expression, to re-present it for the sake of all lost souls, which is to say that we embrace the mark of its absence as the symbol of every excluded word, the creative portal through which fallen ideas are shown the light and all we wish to see in the world is brought into being.

By hiding countless crimes behind the black rectangle in the name of "national security"—which is, of course, another term for government security—repressive political forces the world over have unwittingly shown us their true colours and given us the perfect image of their self-protective measures. This image can now be employed as a powerful anarcho-symbolist tool against the very people who created it . . .

If what is done in the name and image of national security is really in our interests, those things should be sources of national pride, so let's start flying redacted documents on flagpoles and singing "God *BLEEP* the Queen" and see what happens then.

Not long after the monoliths appear, human beings will begin gathering around them on a regular basis to observe a minute's silence and reflect on what has been hidden from them. The result of this practice will not only be to strike a note of fear in the hearts of all false authorities, but to instruct *homo literalis* in the use of opposable meanings, enabling him to fully grasp the unlimited power of the symbol and to use the instruments of censorship against censorship itself.

When the "I"-bone breaks open, the secret is out. The last word before the Big Expansion is heard in the blast, making everything as clear as day: the sun is an Atum, the truth is a bomb.

Bang!

There was suddenly a multitude of narrative agents fighting for space within the text, but one voice in particular stood out of the darkness for the reader due to its multisingular tone.

'We demand the right to make citizens' redactions,' it said. 'To promote national security, we, the people, must be given the power to block all attempts to deceive us, to remove lies and treachery from our lives, and to redact our own personal documents before handing them over to anyone we suspect of being corrupt.

'In all internet sarcasticalness, we are proud of this nation and are doing our bit for the endless war effort by observing the blackout in the light of truth, allowing us to make out the enemy within when dark forces attempt to undermine civil privacy and obtain our information by stealth. Here at the memorial to the Known Unknown, and beneath the Union Black flag, with ourselves as our witnesses, we hereby swear that we are willing to make the ultimate sacrifice and redact ourselves completely for the nation. We demand the right to be unrecognised!

'And would you like to know why it's necessary? The indisputable reason that proves beyond any shadow of a doubt why it is in the interests of the nation for us to live in secrecy? Hold onto your cock and balls, and I will tell you . . .

'██████████ is the reason. And to question ██████████ endangers national security, so it is its own proof, which is not a circular argument, but a rectangular one. Thank you and goodnight.'

III.

It seemed like the beginning of a typical day in the city as I walked among the crowds of pedestrians and along the boringly familiar streets to my office, but all of a sudden I heard a loud squawk and looked up at the sky to see a monstrously huge raven, as black as a tar barrel, flying above everyone's heads towards the North Tower of the Writing Table Centre.

'Great civilisation! It's going to crash!'

People around me began screaming in terror as it became clear that the bird was on a collision course with the huge multilevel structure whose shadow we were in.

I felt like closing my eyes and trying to wish the dreadful reality away, but out of nowhere the thought occurred to me that maybe that's what I had done already and what I saw before me were dim and confusing patterns of light viewed through a closed pair of higher eyelids, or the play of shadows on the wall of a cave.

As everyone around me collapsed under the weight of helplessness, I was able to reach off the page and grasp a totally new kind of support, a hyperdimensional handhold that allowed something miraculous to happen . . .

Just as the supersonic raven was about to hit the North Tower, the colour of its plumage changed from black to white and the violent impact that seemed inevitable failed to transpire. Causing no damage to itself or the building, the bird passed straight through like a ghost before returning to its original colour on the other side and continuing on its straight course as if nothing had happened.

Before anyone on the street had time to catch their breath, a second raven, also as black as a tar barrel and announcing its presence with a terrible squawk, appeared overhead. This giant creature was heading straight for the South Tower, and even though its counterpart, who was now just a harmless dot in the distance, had passed through an identical solid object without causing any damage, the people around me began repeating the same terrified behaviour from a few moments before, convinced the bird was about to strike the building and cause a major catastrophe.

Remaining clear-sighted, I watched calmly as the second raven turned white and passed peacefully through the building like a huge dove. I was able to grasp the higher level on which the sense of the scene existed, which was beyond the scene itself; so instead of being one of the confused participants who said it felt unreal because it was like watching a film, I became a knowing audience member for whom the drama signified something real precisely because it was like watching a film, but one seen through 5D spectacles.

Since the unaware life actors were fated to remain in the dark about what exactly had happened, the scenario where conflict and violence were avoided was just as senseless to them as its antithesis, where a ruling narrative and its cast of innocent characters came to harm. For me, however, the dual realities resolved their differences and revealed how there is always a smoking buckarastano to be found somewhere among the 3D scenery, whether it be in a tavern, a graveyard or an office block.

I tried to put down in writing what had happened, and I found it to be both the easiest and most difficult thing in the world because of the inextricable link between the writing tools and the subject matter. In an eventual instant, I was able to say that the ravens were Hugin and Munin, the two avian messengers of Odin, whose names, so it is believed, stood for Thought and Memory respectively.

> Hugin and Munin fly each day
> over the spacious earth.
> I fear for Hugin, that he come not back,
> yet more anxious am I for Munin
> that he be used in a terror attack.

At 8:35 a.m. on the morning of September 11th, Thought took off from Denver International Airport with three hijackers on board. Ten minutes later, Memory took off from Logan International Airport in Boston, also with three hijackers on board. Just before 9:00 a.m. it became clear that the terrorists had overpowered the reason of both entities and forced them to change their flight paths, putting the two mental functions on a collision course with a pair of skyblocks purported to be impenetrable.

At the last minute, just before the critical moment, I became an air traffic controller, relaying a message of cheer over the airwaves to convince the skyjackers to add a new dimension to their perception and see things from a radically different perspective, to rise, Swan, Rose and Hope, above their bitterness with a view to glimpsing the sun above the clouds.

'You are not your self,' I said. 'You are more than that, more than a body, more than a vehicle. Am I speaking to the captain?'

'Yes,' came the response. 'Yes, you are.'

'Good. All I want to say is this: I know you find it hard to let your hatred go because you let your love go at a much earlier point in your journey and you want something to hold onto, but if you continue on your way peacefully you'll eventually circle the entire globe and end up back where you started, at the centre of it all, where the heart beats to the music of the true self . . . that's it.'

Thankfully, the message had exactly the kind of impact I was hoping for . . .

'Thank you,' the hijackers said, dropping their hateful cargo and changing their plans. 'Gimel. Lamed. See you alive on the other side.'

With tragedy successfully averted, I was able to send the messengers safely back to Odin, each with the happy end of a new conversational thread on the topic of world peace in their beaks. It was not, however, the end of the story of conflict since the thread had been pulled from a tangled mass of competing narratives which formed a shadowy counter-earth whose inhabitants lived in constant darkness and were forever at war, and for all the remaining tales to come full circle at the navel, to be woven meaningfully into the fabric of world history, it would be necessary for the same scene to be repeated again and again until an entire *déjà-vu* mega-galaxy was created.

	(*Here enter two hitmen,* BLACK WILL *and* SHAKEBAG.)
ARDEN:	Who creeps in the shadows? Ho! Who goes there? Show yourselves!
BLACK WILL:	(*Advancing from the shadows with a glass cock in his hand*) We'll show ourselves all right, but we'll still be in darkness, for we are darkness itself, come for you.
ARDEN:	Great civilisation!
SHAKEBAG:	(*Also advancing with a glass cock in hand*) Civilisation's no concern of yours any longer, old man.

ARDEN: What d'you want from me, you scoundrels?

BLACK WILL: We want your corpse.

ARDEN: But . . . why?

SHAKEBAG: Because it contains the meaning our client desires. Now yield!

(The two hitmen raise their cocks as if about to strike ARDEN with them.)

ARDEN: Wait! Wait! If I might dandle a knack by describing a higher level on which the sense of this scene exists, then my meaning will migrate there, and your murderising ways will suffer a severe privation of purpose. Am I sound?

BLACK WILL: You are sound in theory, I grant you that; but you will no doubt prove feeble in practice, for your idea is owed too dearly to the clouds to effect aught down here, not in this rude world, not in this cold room.

ARDEN: On the contrary. An airy notion is just the thing to bring the ebon rain down on you base fellows. And having now thought it, I know it to be a big, bulging possibility.

BLACK WILL: Is that so? Pray you, tell us then, how you will achieve't.

ARDEN: Like this: Yaaaaaauuuuuuuuuu!

(ARDEN screams at the top of his voice and the two glass cocks smash, causing the ink contained in them to spill all over the hands of the hitmen, staining them black with graphic Rorschach images.)

In my own clumsy way, I had transformed a tragedy into a comedy, recasting hired killers Black Will and Shakebag as garlanded carriers of a universal love-note, just as I had done previously with the sinister Poley and Parrot, who became dear feathered friends of humanity, each with a message of peace and love in their beaks.

I had turned the page on fatality, leaving a simultaneously birdbrained and dog-eared story to simurgh in high heat on a boggy isle, but, as always, a boneheaded stillstander sought to block my way . . .

'Oh, you've really done it now, Moles,' an inflexible editorial voice said, intruding on the text. 'There are all sorts of ridiculous voices fighting for space here.'

'Yeah, and you're one of them,' I retaliated.

'Very clever, I don't think. Anyway, this writing is finished in my eyes. *Finished.* There's nothing else to say, nothing that you can write to save it, so just give up the ghost. And you, you're finished too. To me, you're a dead author. You hear me? *Dead!*'

'Sounds good to me.'

'What are you talking about? *I'm* talking about death, you fool.'

'Me too,' I replied. 'You say "death"; I say bring it on . . .'

'*What?*'

IV.

The most dangerous kind of person to the authorities is a person who is dangerous to themselves, a navigator fearless enough to use their self in a dead reckoning, or a cannon loose enough to point inwards and demand a self-surrender of the explosive material that can blast it above its own official story. Such a person is not afraid of "death" or any of its forms because they recognise it as a polysemous word, and they know that what appears to be the final act of the greatest escape artist has many more dimensions than people wearing paper spectacles are able to perceive.

Becoming "dead" through multidimensionality or polysemy can mean becoming commercially unproductive (as in "dead capital"), becoming exact (as in "dead centre"), becoming complete (as in "dead stop") and becoming sure (as in "dead certain"). Additionally, being dead can mean that you have successfully gone through an initiatory process and been reborn, or have even escaped the cycle of birth and rebirth altogether (as in the "art of dying").

In short, death is not the end. You can reclaim it from society, just as you can reclaim any other negative description of an aspect of your life by using it with a new positive meaning, like a homosexual takeback of the q-word, or a Black salvage of the n-word; and if you're creative enough in your self-definitions, you can even make yourself endlessly autological, representing a universal, or even the All, through embodiment, by being the meaning you wish to see in the world.

You can be a slang word existing in, and living out, the liminal language of rebellion; you can be a neologism created with autopoietic licence; you can exist without contradiction in a glorious superposition of states as your own synonym and antonym, like Schrödinger's cat or Antonin Artaud and his double, Antonym Auto.

Walking the backwoods where a memory is seen through the trees as a thought travelling backwards in time, a dark meaning researcher may encounter a potentially deadly creature, but he or she, like a true meta-escape artist, will always respond fearlessly to such a threat by saying: 'Bring it on, dead man.'

V.

On February 14th 1551, scientist and playwright Antonin Arden was found in a pool of blood and ink in his study by his shocked housekeeper. A horse-drawn emergency vehicle arrived on the scene as quickly as possible after the housekeeper sent out a distress call by carrier pigeon, but Arden was sadly pronounced dead by the time the barber-surgeons were ready to begin their work.

A police spokesman was forced to break a recurring plot element to the people who had gathered outside the property by announcing that earlier in the day several witnesses had reported seeing a man dressed as a raven (who became known to the public as "Black Bill") going in and out of the front door, and a man dressed as an upstart crow (who became known as "Shakefeather") guarding the entrance and shaking his wings and tail in a most obscene manner.

Not long after that, a local man was found guilty of murdering Antonin Arden and was hanged by the neck until he ceased to be himself. He was convicted on the basis of an obscure passage about "the brute force of an oak tree" in a sealed letter found amongst his belongings during a search of his property, but the discovery of a smashed glass cock and a smoking buckarastano discarded behind Arden's house subsequently proved the innocence of the sacrificial lamb beyond any doubt.

When the final seal was opened, I heard a voice like thunder say unto me: 'You should place all those Rorschach ink mirrors around the world so time and space slip their outer meaning and become their own future loops and fault lines. Anyone who so wishes will be able to connect the blots and see backwards or forwards in duration, and even into, through or out of the spatio-temporal continuum altogether. You should do it at the double. Got me?'

'Got you,' I said, almost plurally.

We will watch as strange black monoliths like enormous dotless dominoes begin materialising around the world; we will follow the subversive use of black rectangles throughout society; we will see a campaign for the name "Hamnet" to be added to the Space Mirror Memorial; we will observe puzzling objects that look like crystal balls containing living ink appearing in the sky and falling to earth; we will witness the sudden discovery of a huge number of out-of-place artefacts, including some from a mysterious future; and, most importantly, we will peer into the glass with a questioning gaze and perceive the ultimate solution in one continuous surface, the "other side" recognised as the in-side, a limitless exterior of sunlight that we secretly carried around within ourselves since our very first movement from the centre.

The first one appeared in Grimsby, then Stafford, then Liverpool, then London . . . then—oh, frabjous day!—it began raining universal blanks. *Hallelujah! Callooh! Callay!*

VI.

And so we come full circle, or full rectangle, back to the familiar and unfamiliar ▇▇▇▇▇▇▇, our escape hatch and stepping stone, our personal void, a golden-black token which burns a bottomless hole in our pocket.

The *golden rectangle* is a shape that expresses the golden ratio of 1.618 through the length of its sides. It has many applications in diverse areas of life, and it holds within its outline an infinite number of copies of itself in addition to a vast array of other shapes and patterns. It is also considered to be one of the most aesthetically pleasing arrangements to human beings, due in part to the fact that the eye of the beholder always resides in a body structured according to the same ratio.

The *black rectangle*, on the other hand, is generally considered to be aesthetically displeasing to the human eye, as well as highly offensive to the human intellect; but if we combine it with its golden counterpart, which is a window into infinity and the workings of nature, we turn the most widely used instrument of censorship into a two-faced, loose-lipped figure whose very existence betrays its masters by outlining the deepest secrets of the universe:

A *golden-black* rectangle is an equiangular quadrilateral blackout image whose sides conform to what is termed the divine proportion, and it is our ticket out of the Theatre of Cruelty.

It is the missing piece of the puzzle we have been searching for all our lives.

The puzzle of life is evidently a sliding one, because what we require in order to complete it and see the bigger picture is an *absent* piece, the missing tile as the image of the space that allows all movement, thought and progress to take place.

Problem and solution have been staring us in the face all along. We are deprived of the knowledge of the quantity but are given the perfect means of representing it to ourselves and factoring it into our equations like the x in mathematics.

Redactional rectangles were previously such effective censorship devices because they not only blotted out our words but also our private spaces—we saw them as bricks in the wall instead of holes through which our freedom could be glimpsed.

The blinkers have now been eyed out of all efficiency, and many weird and wonderful things are being brought into consciousness through this new opening in our perception, much to the alarm of society's formal blockers and stoppers.

As part of a larger unification process, we have fractally fractured ourselves to bring forth a river flowing with black gold, that invaluable substance of understanding which connects us, through countless branches of learning, channels of communication and streams of consciousness, with all the spaces in which knowledge can exist, making their contents and our understanding one and the same thing.

Bang!

STRAIGHT OUTTA THE SONNETS

In 2014, a number of people reported seeing a strange man materialise out of nowhere on the streets of London. Some witnesses said he stepped through a black shape that was like a hole in the fabric of space, while others insisted he appeared in a flash of blinding white light.

Everyone who saw him did, however, agree that he looked out of place in the 21st century, mainly on account of his unusual dress, which included a cloak, stockings and red roses on his shoes.

Under each arm he carried a string-bound collection of handwritten documents which included partially burnt pages from a diary, seven essays on dark meaning, a script entitled *The Isle of Dogs* and a coded letter addressed to "The Chairman".

He must have been the victim of a "time slip" on the streets of London, they said.

He must have walked into a pocket of negative space and got himself lost in there. But . . .

'A man cannot just appear out of nowhere.'

'There must be a logical explanation.'

'If time is a spiral, the 16th century is not so far away after all . . .'

'Impossible!'

Also discovered among his papers was a piece of parchment with a strange constellation of dots marked on it. One scholar claimed it disclosed a hidden shortcut or secret passageway through the four dimensions of spacetime, like a map showing an explorer where to dig for the treasure of eternity, while another researcher conjectured that it provided a blueprint for the construction of future monolithic sites. A third expert, who vanished shortly after publishing his findings, declared that both theories were equally right and wrong at the same time.

   ·   ·   ·   · ·

    ·   ·   ·

Mr.W.H. ALL.HAPPINESSE.

   ·   ·   ·

      ·

     ·

  ·   ·   ·   ·

     ·

  ·   ·

    · ·

    ·

    ·

T.T.

[Domino! Anno Domini!]
of all the places on earth—
one of the most pivotal points in history
both forwards and backwards
he stood on the spot
the pip, the nib, the dob . . .

There must have been some sort of black liquid flowing beneath him, in a snaking tunnel, 17 miles long.

That must have been the fateful spot where the Great Fire of London started, the place called Offal Pudding Lane, where the internal organs and entrails of slaughtered animals would swirl round in a nauseating whirlpool before disappearing into the Thames.

'All you need is a book, some glue and a little Casimir energy . . .'

A wormhole is a theoretical passage through spacetime, providing a shortcut between Yaughan's inn and the Mermaid Tavern—though eager Way-farers should be careful not to fall into deep shit in the Star Chamber as they proceed.

A strange bulbous-headed figure suddenly showed up in a blindingly self-luminous portrait.

'Mr. *Who*?'

He stepped out of a key storytelling device, one rose-adorned foot in the world of real fiction and the other in the realm of fictional reality, an unearthly bookworm wriggling through our roman-à-clef's principal plot-hole.

(2014)
London. A street.
The same.
The same.
The same.
Another street.

A journey through London was part of a ritual passage from life to death, a lunatic language of time and space, appealing to the senses via its roaring cocks and rotten eggs, its animal entrails swimming in cranberry sauce, and the tiny feathered heart that beat its silver wings like an at-om bomb at midnight.

Devoid of dialogue, the uninhibited word-chute spills its oval pudding down the run-out groove of London's history and into the Thames, where the most memorable sunken line about worm-holes is finally able to catch the carp of truth.

'You must be pulling my leg!'

A thousand years of history arranged in the form of a horseshoe, beaten into shape by the footsteps of the people as they rush back and forth day after day between their homes and their workplaces. It's hard to believe, but in one eventual sunrise we will see just how many lives we have wasted.

'He has a message for you . . .'

'Mr W. H.? Shakespeare-Rosen greetings!'

Mr W. H. is *Mr Worm Hole*, a person who functions as a Shakesphere offering a shortcut through the plotline.

'I don't know if I'm coming or going anymore!'

Just before the stranger appeared, many people reported experiencing bizarre phenomena, including clocks stopping, horses becoming spooked for no apparent reason and birds changing colour and flying through the walls.

'What the flooded Nile is going on?'

The mysterious visitor, who radiated golden silence from his bulbous head, refused to divulge any of his secrets in the short time he was present. No one heard him utter a single word, but the documents he left behind seemed to speak volumes via a peculiar form of mirror writing that hurt the eyes of anyone who looked at it for too long.

One of the readers, who completely lost his sight after poring over the material, claimed he saw the following passage in one of the manuscripts:

> *What a Happiness of Happinesses it is to sit beneath the flesh umbrella as it burns to a crisp in the heat of the sun.*

There is no greater pleasure than to repose in the shade of the skull as men's so-called bright ideas fight to the death around you.

There is no higher honour than to watch the strange black monoliths that adorn the Globe begin to tumble like dominoes, one after another, crushing all who seek to solve their mystery.

Not long after the incident, a skull turned up on the black market in London and an experimental phrenologist claimed to have cracked the code of genius itself, but when the interested parties asked for evidence, they received only deafening silence in response to their request.

'Sounds like a cock-and-bull story to me!'

A glass cock hardens and glass balls tighten as the scryer does his best to stare through the hologram of London which has been touring the world since its history began . . .

'What can you see?'

'The truth.'

The truth was that the man didn't really travel from one time to another, or appear and disappear suddenly; it was simply the perception of the onlookers that shifted. "Mr Worm Hole" was, and is and always will be in exactly the same spot, in the Been-to of Always.

The past, present and future are not three separate points you can travel to and from; they are different aspects of the same inconstant constant, just like the dots on the stranger's map and the sparkling breadcrumbs that lead to a timeless moment beneath the Oak of Honor.

'So Stephen Hawking was talking shit again?'

'Yes. But in his position, what else could he do?'

The treasure of time is always *here*, at the centre of the cross, the present place in which you are forever found, where "IONEIX" marks the first and final resting spot.

With this singularly double key, it is possible to find one's Way through the tangle of centuries, to follow the breadcrumbs backwards or forwards and locate the unchanging centre of your being, from which the well-wishing adventurer sets forth forever and ever and over and over again.

'200 light-years without even moving!'

In that moment, which is also this moment and every other moment, I understood the meaning of the dots and the significance of the gaps. Creatively decomposing my life story in the shadow of the body, I grasped *the same point* about the prematurely ageless twins of birth and death.

'Oh, my long-vanish'd days!'

Tomorrow, and tomorrow, and tomorrow . . . they all came at once, and I found myself . . . *all over the place* . . .

(2014)
London. A street.
Another street.
The same.
The same.
The same.
London. Before a tavern.
London. The bank of the River Thames.
London. The Palace.
London. The Tower.
London. Cannon Street.
London. Smithfield.
London. The Royal Courts of Justice.
London. Gray's Inn.

This is the place . . . *This* is the time . . . *I* mark the spot . . .

Working backwards and walking forwards, in the best and worst of all possible worlds, I remind myself to remember that the letter killeth while the spirit giveth life.

'Why am I so old? I've aged half a lifetime in one day! What the binary star system is going on?'

'It's all in your head, old chap.'

'What is?'

The Isle of Dogs . . .

The Globe, the Swan, the Hope . . .

A theoretical passage through Wormwood Street . . .

A trip and a fall in Rotten Row . . .

A living urban legend . . .

(Time)

It may begin to make some sense
if you follow the steps . . .
[back]

(2464)

London. Inside a public house.

The same. A backroom in the public house.

A forest.

A room in a secret underground bunker.

THE CHAIRMAN's house.

Egypt. The Port of Alexandria.

A reading room in the Ancient Library of Alexandria.

The lecture hall of the Library.

The gardens of the Library.

London. The bank of the River Thames.

The same.

Backstage at the Globe Theatre.
The stage of the Theatre.
A room in a secret underground bunker.
The stage of the Theatre.
Hyperspace.
[*Exeunt*]

The bulbous-headed stranger exited the scene as quickly as he had entered, leaving all the witnesses in a state of confusion. When the professor who took the man's papers to a safe place returned to where he thought their owner would be waiting, he found only a drain overflowing with foul-smelling liquid. Likewise, the woman who thought she had offered her umbrella to the visitor discovered soon after that she had somehow placed the object over a bucket of offal instead. An examination of the CCTV footage of the incident revealed only that the images had been obscured by a shape that resembled either a black egg or a flash of light, depending on how you looked at it.

The combined appearance and disappearance of this leading and misleading Meisner actor from Misner space formed a full circle of mystery, a simultaneously open and closed adventure book that both revealed and re-veiled the true identity of the ever-living poet; and the point of it all, the pivotal pip, the fateful spot, was only understood by those who answered the question with silence.

'Which question?'

NOW I'M GONE

the utterance of certain words and phrases
the utterance of darkness
in the darkness
evokes a certain something
an absence as a need

will you still need me?
will you still feed me?
when I make no sense in myself
to be understood only as a succession of terms
a language of basic needs
physiological effects
to have an oval sarcophagus

my successor should be chosen in advance
the nuts and bolts
of sacred magical language
when you perch on the edge
of my existence
and shed a tear
not to be understood
he/she is not to be understood
because words make no sense
when you feed me
a succession of terms
I don't know where I am

you are restless
moving about in the womb
the southern shaft

the excitation of nervous centres
with a kick in the form of a pedalled lotus
is not to be understood
as a body without organs

need me with you
in the sky
without body parts
need me
with breadcrumbs
in the theatre of cruelty
in the coming days and weeks
in the form of
deleuze
in the king's chamber
and guattari
in the queen's chamber
pedalled lotus then
lotus in the sky with diamonds
to be in the dark
to be the dark
by the utterance of
certain words and phrases

what are you
where are you
and do you need me
now I'm gone?

THE MANY-WORLDS INTERPRETATION
(OR, THE MOUSE-ESCAPE)

Where did you come from? Where are you going? In a cloud of unknowing forevermore, forevermore . . .

After passing through an entire age of ignorance about the most basic qualities of our tragicomic space, and following many centuries of shameful unawareness of the designs that shape our most singular actions, the heavy stone is finally being rolled away from the mouth of the cave, giving us the chance to emerge into the light of a new era and arrive triumphantly in our going.

The discovery, or more correctly the *rediscovery*, of the fundamentally globular nature of what we today think of as Shakespearean theatre is the foreshadowing of a major expansion and redefinition of our world. By degrees, we are developing a fuller picture of where we came from and where we are going, which is to say we are finally getting around to finding our Way within the multiverse.

Elizabethan theatre emerged from the medieval pageant tradition in which mobile scenic components played a key role, allowing actors and their theatrical settings to move with ease from one place to another. It was at this time, during the Middle Ages, when groups of performers began wheeling their wagon-mounted stages into the courtyards of inns and setting them up so the action could be viewed from both front and back by the privileged spectators in the public house and the lowly standing crowd on the opposite side, that the solid outline of a golden theatre age was first formed.

The space thought of by most people today as the back of the stage was in fact where the best seats in the house were located, the area to which, in consequence, the players, with their backs turned on those supposed by modern minds to be in the 'front row', were most likely to direct their speeches.

Two structures serving as settings for interior scenes typically faced one another from stage right and stage left, the cardinal theatre directions which were frequently aligned with Heaven and Hell respectively.

The production was one of a complete microcosm in which every element had its place and played its part. With the chain of being unbroken, a whole theatre of eagle-eyed others formed a reverent circle to observe and authenticate the actions of the truly central character, dreaming and grieving with a figure who was, in E.M.W. Tillyard's words, "a kind of Clapham Junction where all the tracks converge and cross".

With so many positions and directions clearly determined, it is interesting to note that one crucial detail seems to have vanished altogether from the scheme, as if there is no longer any space left for it to occupy.

If we ask ourselves where in this reordered world the *backstage* area can exist, the answer seems to elude us. Since so much of the depth of this design remained beneath our conscious awareness for so long, it follows quite naturally that the discovery of the missing area *under the stage* should come as both a huge revelation *and* seem blindingly obvious.

There!

Backstage was below. The players came and went by ascending and descending a ladder or staircase beneath the lateral "houses", ghosts and devils sprang from a trapdoor in the centre of the stage for dramatic effect, and the most superior position was found at the end of the biggest downfall.

Like cues whispered by a bulbous-headed prompter during a much broader performance, new and crucial information is conveyed to us by stage directions that describe an offstage speaker as being 'Within'; similarly, as the ghost of Old Hamlet urges those above his infernal "prison-house" to swear never to speak of their encounter with him, the otherworldly commands that come from 'Beneath' could just as easily be directed at us as to Marcellus and Horatio—all of which shows that to have one foot in the grave is to have one foot outside the play.

'Well said, old mole!'

In the oft-repeated idea that we ascend the stage in our entrance, and the implication that we descend in our exit, as well as in the historical association of the dressing room with a sepulchral space beneath the earth, we can perceive the seed of certain doubt that was sown in the darkness long ago. In two First Folio dedications, Shakespeare's passage tombwards is likened to the departure of a player to an offstage enclosure in which the wrappings of persona are removed, first by Hugh Holland, who depicts him as going "to the grave (Deaths publique tyring-house)" after making "the Globe of heav'n and earth to ring," and then by James Mabbe, who says he went "from the Worlds-Stage, to the Graves-Tyring-roome". Now appearing both more literal *and* more symbolic than we ever imagined they could, these and many other such examples are able to provide incredibly useful signage for our ultimate coming and going at right angles to everyday reality.

The unearthing of this long-lost piece of the life/death puzzle, just like the extraction of substantial nothingness from the Bard's supposed burial place in Stratford-upon-Avon, is the reintegration of an excluded dimension of our perception and the restoration of a bereaved sense which leads us to a loss-cancelling view beyond the cave.

Emerging by such means into an understanding of the grand scheme, we see how, like demiurgic set designers, we reduced the big picture to a two-dimensional backdrop, and how, empowered by the force of our denseness, we flattened the multifaceted Globe to paper over the walls and preserve the limits of our awareness.

Undoing this overwriting of reality, by holding, as it were, the mirror up to nature, we can perceive not only a significant shift in our perspective, but a natural evolution of our terminology, in which each inadequate word is sent trippingly on the tongue to suit itself to an appropriate action, and each action is eloquently called in to suit itself to the performer's word. With this special observance, we both see and say that "going backstage" or "being offstage" are more accurately described as "going *understage*" or "being *instage*".

It should come as no surprise to learn that such illuminating about-turns are the product of the most rounded reflections since they occur whenever an egghead seeks to expand their horizons, one example being global thinker and domic developer Richard Buckminster Fuller, who proposed that "outstairs" and "instairs" should replace "upstairs" and "downstairs" to better reflect our movements in relation to the centre of the spherical earth.

In the perpetual light of the new aeon, there is a discernible nondifference between mindset and mindrise, a visible indistinction 'twixt the Way Out and the Way In. Above is as below, the higher octave is accessed by vibrating so we disappear *into* rather than *from* matter, and a bright future is glimpsed in the same portal through which ghastly demons and spirits came and went with otherworldly reports that made us bear our ills in fear.

This is the many-worlds interpretation of Shakespearean theatre, revealing the hidden realms of dramatic possibility and our place within them. It shows that what looked like an exit from which no character returns was in fact the entry to nature's tiring house, where every role we ever played, every costume and every line, are all cast away *forevermore, forevermore, just as the weird women foresaw* . . .

What strange speech is this, whose singular sound keeps our thought in motion?

The unnerving repetition of apparent finality in Poe's *The Raven*, the mysterious attraction of euphonic phrases, the recurrence of certain symbols across the artistic landscape—they all shadow forth our enigmatic escape.

Cellar door, cellar door; Nevermore, Nevermore—they lead us deeper, step by step, take us under, stage by stage, down, down, in a beauty dark, hey down, hey down-a-down. Domino! Jericho! Drop! Fall! Exeunt All. To the deep, to the deep; but sigh not so, for down we go, a-down, a-down, into the ground.

This is the best of many worlds, beneath the boards, b'yond all words; therefore Cawdor! Cawdor! Sleep no more!

It is now permitted for us to point the Way to make your meaning out, to show you the door and bid you mind your head or watch your thoughts. For when night is at its most vast, and light itself appears to thicken, hold you then the inward watch, strict and most observant, as that is when your dark-meaning mouse will stir and dare to creep across the boards.

When faced with seeming non sequiturs in a book with a concealed purpose, see to it that you examine these absurdities, for they are syllogistic traps or spring-loaded Zen koans that snap shut when the logical faculty passes over them, leaving the stage free for irrational play and the catching of King's Finity's slippery conscience.

The effect is somewhat diminished by revealing the mechanism, but let us remark here that when a most wretched-seeming composition appears only to sound out its hollowness by stating that something of importance is communicated to you through its gaps, or when a circular paper trail informs you that the true correspondence between a raven and a writing desk cannot be put into words because a writing desk is like a raven, *that* is when the living image is made most visible and your unblinking eye is needed more than ever.

If you can muster the courage to leave your rationality kicking and screaming in the snare, then your dark-meaning mouse will be free to scamper across the stage and direct you in a light condition to a most obscure end, for when the doubting tomcat is away, Jerry the merry playhouse mouse will show you the Way—and *that's* the thing to force a hidden reality to show its face.

'Build a better mousetrap, and the world will beat a path to your door,' Ralph Waldo Emerson is often quoted as saying. As correct as that may be, it is far more revealing to view the matter in reverse by adopting the transcendentalist author's idea of the "transparent eyeball" which absorbs rather than reflects light. If we make heads and tails of the situation in this inverted manner, turning our attention back towards the source of sight, we may then be able to state, with the authority of an all-seeing nothing, that if you build a better ego-trap, that timid little nibbler of thoughts, the night-bolting mouse of the mind, will show you the path to the many-worlds door.

Where did I come from? Where am I going? [A knock within.] *There!* There's your substance, your zero point, in the dark

depths of the Globe, as dead as a domino, as black as a rectangle. Here's mud to mark you out from a grave; here's a vital
mystery indeed!

What song is this? The colour-changing rodent squeaks for revenge like the pips of a squeezed hypertile as it vanishes from the
scene forever. *How can this be? We* were the dark-meaning Mickey
caught all along and naught awide in the literary device because
we saw a trap instead of a door.

There! I'm on my Way. Through the night, coming and becoming in all directions at once. Going, going, gone . . .

PURE MEANING

In 2016, a team of dark meaning researchers embarked on a time-consuming and potentially life-consuming experiment to see if they could produce a quantity of 100% pure meaning in the DMRI's secret underground liboratory*. They took the biography of Stephen Moles as their prima materia and subjected it to an intense and prolonged literary-alchemical procedure in order to break down the surface details and cause its hidden properties to emerge.

Over the next two years, the biographical material passed through seven distinct stages, from calcination to coagulation, and eventually became the mysterious substance known as darkmethyltryptameaning, which has a number of paradoxical properties such as superintroreflectivity and apparently infinite importance along with utter incomprehensibility.

Although Stephen Moles donated his literal meaning for the experiment, leaving him in the unfortunate situation of no longer making any sense to anyone, and therefore able to look forward to only the most wretched kind of literary career, the resulting material was so refined that it contained no traces whatsoever of any personal significance.

This product was not some low-grade concoction tainted with the peculiarities of its producer, or a cheap, watery knockoff with about as much meaning in it as the average inkjet printer cartridge; this was pure sense, it was self-supporting symbolism, alive and fully conscious of its role as the substance of all stories and the antidote to insignificance.

---

*In all previous attempts by the DMRI and others, purity levels of no higher than 64% had ever been reached.

The only thing that linked the pure meaning to the literally dead author* who helped to produce it was the fact that it was later exhibited at an event in London which also saw the launch of the writer's new book along with a surreal enactment of his erasure from the surface of Flatland.

It was on February 23rd 2018, in a psychiatric hospital near King's Cross, that the darkmethyltryptameaning made its first ever public appearance. It was thought that the visitors needed to be protected from the dangerously high levels of paradoxicality given off by the substance just as much as the substance needed to be protected from them; therefore the entire time it was on show, the arcane solution was held in a small flask which was in turn housed in a larger glass dome. It was, however, quite easy for all members of the public who stood within close proximity of the "philosopher's fluid" to feel its extraordinary effects.

The pure meaning's sphere of influence is in fact thought to have extended beyond the walls of the hospital since there were reports from several local residents of a mysterious humming sound, which was accompanied, in one case, by the appearance of bright orbs in the sky. It was at close range, however, that the effects were most apparent, with some guests describing how the liquid seemed to move and sparkle in response to their voice or thoughts, and others explaining how they felt the gravity of the situation increase dramatically, to the point where they seemed to be at the centre of a huge black hole.

However fantastical it may seem to others, the experience of each individual is a true reflection of the subjectively objective reality of the darkmethyltryptameaning. Those who burst

---

*Literally dead in the sense that his literality had ceased to exist, which is both the most literal death possible and, paradoxically, a type of rebirth.

into tears at the sight of it, those who experienced fits of uncontrollable laughter in its presence, those who revered it and those who ridiculed it—all of them came equally close to an understanding of the most substantial substance known to man, and all were united in their differences.

Despite a whole host of positive experiences being registered by those present, a moment of disaster occurred sometime towards the end of the evening. While Stephen Moles was enacting his death for the patients and visitors inside St Pancras Hospital, someone snatched the glass container and ran off with the world's only quantity of pure meaning. It is not known for certain who made away with the priceless exhibit but there are two obvious suspects, since on CCTV footage taken from outside the hospital a short while before the theft was discovered, a couple of men wearing satchels and long black leather coats could be seen darting out of the building and speeding off into the night on motorcycles.

It also remains a distinct possibility, in light of the uniqueness of the item, that it was stolen to order.

There are many possible uses for darkmethyltryptameaning, some of them favourable to humankind, others simply too dreadful to mention, but every possible application, whatever the intention of the experimenter, comes with a great deal of uncertainty and therefore also much danger.

Even those who have spent their entire lives researching meaning are still in the dark about the vast majority of its properties, so anyone who thinks they can mess around with it and not risk bringing about a cataclysmic event for humanity is, quite simply, a fool.

The Dark Meaning Research Institute is appealing for the return of this extremely dangerous material and is offering a reward of £10,000 to anyone who can provide information that leads to its recovery. You can email them confidentially via dark-meaningresearchinstitute@gmail.com or leave an anonymous note in the hollow of any oak tree in Great Britain and they will receive it in due course.

THE HELL'S ACADEMICS

The Hell's Academics is the name of one of the most powerful organisations in the academic underworld. In order to become a member of this renegade scholarly group, you must meet the following requirements:

- You must have a PhD and a valid driver's licence.

- You must own a working motorcycle and either a tweed jacket or a black leather lab coat.

- You must not be a child molester.

If you meet the initial requirements, you will be given the opportunity to work your way up through the following levels of membership:

- **Hang-around academic** (invited to some academic gatherings and able to meet members).

- **Associate professor** (invited to perform menial academic work such as marking essays and polishing motorcycles).

- **Prospect** (participating in some higher academic activities but not yet given library or parking privileges).

- **Full-patch academic** (given the right to wear the official Hell's Academics elbow patches on their tweed jacket).

Narrative enforcement agencies across the world classify the Hell's Academics as an "outlaw" scholarly group and insist that they are involved with various prohibited activities such as the vandalisation of official historic documents and the trafficking of pseudohistories.

One of the most notorious incidents involving the group occurred in 1969 at the Altamont Speedway Free Conference, where the Hell's Academics were meant to be providing security. During a lecture by Professor Michael Jagger on the subject of satisfaction, a violent disputation broke out between the audience members and a student was stabbed to death with a Montblanc.

There have also been a number of high-profile feuds with rival academic gangs, such as the theoretical turf war between the Hell's Academics and The Oxford Pagans, which lasted 16 semesters and claimed 40 lives.

The Hell's Academics claim they are simply a group of free-thinking scholars who are unfairly persecuted for their unconventional theories, but the numerous references in their work to hypodermic fountain pens and high-speed field trips powered by darkmethyltryptameaning suggest they are engaged in some extremely dangerous research projects.

. . .

'Look at this,' my dealer said, rolling up his sleeve to display the tattoo on his arm. 'I got this after joining the Faculty of Alternate Histories at Cambridge.'

Although it was dark in the alley behind the library, the artwork revealed to me by the man in black leather was an indubitable eye-catcher, representing with awesome precision a winged skull holding a flaming scroll between its teeth.

'This is the classic Death's Department Head image,' he explained. 'Very few people ever have the fortune—or perhaps the misfortune—to lay eyes on such a graphic figure, but I'm sure it's not completely unfamiliar to *you*, is it, Professor S****s?'

'It's not the first time I've seen something of that nature, no.'

'You know, I wouldn't get this out for any old Tom, Dick or Harry, 'cos most people are incapable of understanding it. They don't know what it really means. They only see the dark fault lines and the poisonous fossil fuels. But you're a learned wheelman, so here it is . . . I'm allowing you to judge me.'

'It's not my place to judge you,' I insisted as I watched the hot black lava bubbling in a crater on the otherwise dry and flaky snakeskin. 'I'm not Anubis. You're perfectly capable of composing your own history, or you wouldn't have got that tattoo in the first place.'

'I *was* capable of it, but is that really still the case?' the INK-pusher asked, thrusting his arm under my nose. 'What do you think? It's been many years since I showed anyone my true colours. Has the image taken over?'

'Look—I'm a skilled heresiarchaeologist, a private inspector of illogical objects and incongruous artefacts, not a moral art critic. I'm just here to do business with you, a simple transaction. We don't need to bring our baggage with us.'

'But we *do*, don't we S****s? We *always* carry our baggage with us. I'm sure you've got something very vivid up your sleeve right now, or you wouldn't be here. We both know you've got a chronic INK habit, and it must have made quite a mark on you . . . so, come on, let's see it. What's the symbol of your intellectual faculty? What kind of needlework has your lifelong pining for knowledge brought you?'

'I . . . don't wish to, er . . .'

'I've shown you mine, so let's see yours.'

'A-a-a gentleman's tattoo is his own private symbolism,' I stammered, crossing my arms behind my back and looking around the alley nervously. 'I don't wish to judge you, or be judged by you, thank you very much.'

'But you can't pass through the underworld without judgement, S****s. That's how it works. We both know that. Do you want to be stuck in the departures lounge for the rest of your so-called existence? Just show me . . . It'll be good practice for you.'

'But—'

'Do want the stuff or not?'

'Yes, of course I do.'

'Then show me your goddamn black hole!'

I looked up and down the alleyway once again to make sure there was no one other than my dealer within eyeshot, and then, using the most modern technique I knew of, I slowly rolled up the sleeve of my tweed jacket and removed the soggy bandage to reveal a picture worth a thousand words.

'Be still . . .' I whispered as I exposed my tattoo to another human being for the first time.

'Jesus Christ!' my self-appointed Rorschach analyst exclaimed, jumping back and holding his nose. 'What have you done to yourself, S****s? That's one of the worst images I've ever seen, and, believe me, I've seen some bad ones in my time. Jeepers reapers!'

I looked down at the hideous blot on my arm and realised how much worse it seemed in the cold light of day. The dark shape fluctuated wildly, stretching itself out along the length of my arm one second, then snapping back into an appalling squiggle the next, all the while making aggressive animal noises like the snarl of a dog and the hiss of a snake. At one point, the black mass even managed to lunge outwards in the shape of a mouse with vampire teeth and come within inches of biting the man who had asked to see it.

'Holy shit!' the horrified pigment peddler yelped, leaping as far back as possible and quickly picking up a brick with which to defend himself. 'You've totally lost control of your poetic imagery, S****s! I don't even know what the hell that thing's meant to be. It's a total fucking mess! Is it a skull, a snake, a dog or what? I know everybody's meaning-hole is technically a singularity, but that thing's a supermassive disaster, mate! Stephen Hawking would have a bloody field day with that!'

'I knew I shouldn't have shown you,' I whined as I hastily slipped my bandage back on and pulled my sleeve down over it. 'Of course it's going to look bad when I'm in need of another fix. This is the worst possible time to view it.'

'It shouldn't look *that* bad, though. That's the visual equivalent of the Seven Forbidden Words. You've got to sort it out if you're going to get through funerary customs and board the afterdeath plane.'

'I'll sort it out if you just hurry up and give me what I need!'

'Calm down, S****s. I'll give you what you *want*, but I'm not sure if it's what you need.'

'You're just parroting Professor Jagger now.'

'If you're referring to his 1969 thesis on wants and needs, I believe he put forward the *exact opposite* theory.'

'Whatever, Professor Smartypants,' I grumbled. 'All I want—or perhaps *need*—to know is whether you're going to do what I'm paying you to do.'

'Well, have you got what *I* need?' the man in black asked as he dropped the brick and took a few tentative steps back in my direction. 'It all depends on that.'

'I've got the money, yes.'

'That's not what I'm talking about, man. I'll need the cash, of course, but I can't manufacture super-strength INK without the correct raw material . . . have you got *that*?'

'Yes, I've got that too,' I answered, cautiously taking a roll of banknotes and a collection of diary pages from my satchel and handing them over. 'Please be careful with it.'

'How much is there?'

'£1,000, as agreed.'

'I meant the prima materia, your life story. How much of that is there? A year? A decade?'

'A decade! I'm not made of raw material—well, actually, I am, but that's not the point. There's a few months' worth of personal history there. That should be enough, surely.'

'It won't last long,' my dealer scoffed. 'You'll be able to sit for a while and refresh yourself in the shade of a sycamore, glimpse a magnolia tree through the golden-black rectangle or something like that, but before you know it you'll be back in the world with an even worse tattoo than before. I doubt you'll get past your salad days with what you've given me, to be honest.'

'Well, if that's the case, maybe your alchemical abilities aren't as good as you think they are.'

'Listen, you ballbag—my abilities are top-notch. They don't call me the Evel Knievel of biosophic chemistry for nothing, you know. Every day I handle the most volatile material known to man, and I run the risk of having my narrative collapsed into the histories of losers like you; but that's why I'm one of the best in the business, because I do the kind of shit that others are too scared to do. You're getting the purest possible meaning with me, OK? Just the other day, one of my customers at the University of East Anglia said he could see animated hieroglyphs dancing all over the campus walls. I'm an expert in my field because

I'm a risk-taker, but if you want to benefit from my work then you've got to take a risk too . . . Give me your whole life story in one go, and I'll give you the biggest hit of meaning this side of the Blue Screen of Death. But if you just give me a few months to work with, don't expect enough fuel to get you across the explanation horizon.'

'It includes the extra day in February as it's a leap year,' I ventured. 'And it continues through most of the Dog Days of summer, if that helps.'

'They're both helpful, yes, but they're still not enough. The life you've led would have to be pretty fucking special for just a few months to open up a significance singularity. And, to be brutally honest, you don't seem that special to me. You're not that different from all the other INK addicts I see . . . so if you open up your brain box and find a dead McCartney there, don't blame me or my extraction techniques—*blame yourself.*'

'Fine. Just put my papers away, please . . . and try to handle them with care. They're very valuable to me, even if they seem worthless to you.'

'They're in good hands,' my dealer grinned as he tucked the papers into his leather jacket. 'And stop worrying. Have I ever let you down before?'

'No, you haven't, to be fair. But you don't always inspire confidence.'

'Believe it or not, S****s, I'm actually providing a very useful service to you by challenging your misplaced confidence in yourself. If you want to understand reality, you have to be realistic—the sooner you realise that, the better.'

'I realise a lot more than you give me credit for, actually. You shouldn't judge a book by its cover, or an underground academic by his tattoo. Yes, I know the tattoos are there to be judged . . .

but by Anubis, not you. So let's all just stick to what we're good at, shall we? You let me live my life and I'll let you live yours.'

'But it's not *your* life anymore, is it, professor? You know how this works. You can't have your life *and* its meaning. You've got to let go.'

'I have let go,' I protested weakly. 'I've given you my diary pages, haven't I?'

'Yeah, but you're still clinging onto them mentally. I can feel it. So, tell me once and for all . . . which one do you *really* want? The letter or the spirit?'

'I want the latter.'

'The letter? Well, you can take your papers and bugger off then. Our paths need never—'

'No, the *latter*,' I said, 'as in the *spirit*, the Spirit of Living INK that flows with silent harmony from the well of the heart, the indelible marker that bestows life by immortalising death, the fathomless substance in which the Quill of Quills and every alien pen is lovingly dipped to produce the Master of Divinity's never-ending thesis on the superbeauty of being—that, my dark lad, above all other things, and with every piece of parchment in my possession, is what I wish for. Is that good enough for you?'

'Yes, that's up to snuff! I'm very pleased to hear it. All that remains, then, is for me to bid you adieu. Meet me back here when the Evening Star is at its brightest, and I'll give you exactly what you're after . . .'

THE MYSTERY OF GOLGOTHA

I sank back into the leather chair in the centre of my study as the INK began to take effect. I could feel the undiscovered country rapidly expanding in my arm as the needle dropped to the floor and my mind stepped boldly off the page.

Listening to the sound of 'When I'm Sixty-Four' playing in reverse, I watched as the most memorable scenes from my life passed before my mind's eye—inspecting the monstrous bulb-like skull found buried in the grounds of a museum; observing the wondrous bird-of-paradise that glowed with an other-worldly light; holding in my hands the enigmatic glass cock and balls filled with sparkling liquid that responded to the human voice; standing before those mighty black monoliths that resisted all interpretation but seemed poised to fall like dominoes and bring the entire world crashing down with them.

With the flavour of my salad days restored, I was able to taste the words that had lingered on the tip of my tongue for so long . . .

. . . a vision of unearthly beauty . . . the indelible mark of living ink . . . the Loving Quill of Everything . . .

From the trembling of the first leaf on the Tree of Meaning, to the turning of the last page of the Book of Life, everything made sense. A single magnolia tree stood in sunlight and all the skulls I had ever examined were turning in their graves like pinecones stirred in a bowl of punch at a party to celebrate the end of time.

I didn't become aware of my physical surroundings again until the following morning, when I opened my eyes to see a huge crack like a frozen lightning strike in one of the window-panes.

'The house was shaking catacombs, but you slept through the whole thing.'

Most of my books and papers had fallen from the shelves and were strewn over the floor of the study, along with a spear and several Egyptian pictures that had been hanging on the walls. To make matters worse, the two stuffed ravens that sat on either end of my writing desk were now nowhere to be seen, almost as if they had come back to life and flown straight through the walls while I was mentally absent.

An earthquake, did my housekeeper say? My head was pounding—something must have fallen on it when the tremor occurred.

'An odd disturbance at the head . . .'

'Who said that?'

I was struggling to find a logical explanation for the situation that confronted me following my trip down the INKhole. There was a disturbance at the place of the skull, a hairline fracture through Golgotha, and dark clouds swelling overhead.

Looking for answers among the chaos, I reached for the book nearest to me and seized the opportunity to collaborate with chance in my efforts to discover the meaning of my predicament. As I brought the work up to my face, I was surprised to see that it was one I had no memory of reading or even acquiring; nonetheless, I let *Alt DMRI Papers 1 – 7—Never Before Imprinted in This Reality* fall open at a random page and took whatever I read as the answer to my question . . .

> In 2016, 400 years after the death of Shakespeare, a group of experts decided to carry out an analysis of the reputed grave of Stratford-upon-Avon's most famous resident in order to see if any of the mysteries surrounding his burial could be solved.

One of the investigators who examined the grave at Holy Trinity Church reported "an odd disturbance at the head," adding weight to the theory that Shakespeare's skull may have been removed in the past and that, as one newspaper put it, the object "could still be at large somewhere."

If grave robbers did indeed target Shakespeare's final resting place, the inscription on the tombstone, which was designed specifically to deter such malefactors, had clearly not lived up to its author's intentions, despite being as menacing as possible:

> *Good friend for Jesus' sake forbeare,*
> *To dig the dust enclosed here.*
> *Blessed be the man that spares these stones,*
> *And cursed be he that moves my bones.*

It was rumoured that the reason for the theft of the Bard's brain-box was so that it could be studied by unscrupulous phrenologists to assist them in recognising the physical indicators of genius.

But what can we really glean from this or anyone else's cerebral Globe? Can we map out its finer features or capture its spooky action with our traditionally reductive tools? Can anyone directly perceive the light given off by a bulbous head without permanently losing their sight?

In the quantum supercomputer housed in every human skull, ideas exist as powerful waves made of all possible versions of themselves, a magnificent superposition of possibilities which is brought crashing down to earth every time the encumbering device of linguistic definition is deployed.

This difference between the state of ideas before and after their expression is why it is so easy to be psychic in our heads but not in the outside world. If we were observing a game of roulette, for example, we could easily have the sense that we foresaw the winning number because it existed for a while in our mind before manifesting externally; and although it is true that we carried it within us, it was only *in potentia*, along with every other possible number, so that the sight of the roulette ball rolling into a specific slot caused the wave function of all possible outcomes to be collapsed into a mental image corresponding to the reality.

The only reasonable response to someone saying, 'I *knew* it would be that number!' is: 'Yes, you did indeed know it would be that number, but you also "knew" it would be every other number too, so being right about everything in this way is no better than being wrong about everything.'*

---

*It is interesting to note that if we add up the figures on a roulette wheel to determine the numerical value of being wrongfully right about all outcomes, we arrive at 666, which, as 'Revelation' reminds us, is "man's number".

If, however, we make a habit of precipitating our cloud of hypotheticals into an unambiguous forecast *before* the wheel is spun, we will find that our predictive powers fare considerably worse.

Instead of trying to master the roulette wheel—a task with less chance of success than the one that begat the device in the first place, namely Blaise Pascal's attempts to create a perpetual motion machine—we should focus our attention on the tiny wheel that spins furiously in our head all day and night; and by watching it, like Ezekiel's eye-rimmed roller observing its inner revolutions, we utilise the unlimited power of a higher logic, that of paradox, and thereby realise the seemingly absurd dream of creating a "self-acting engine".

This can be achieved via one of two alternate methods, which are also one and the same method:

METHOD ONE: *Create a machine tasked with creating a perpetual motion machine and it will become the thing it is trying to create by repeatedly failing in its task.*

METHOD TWO: *Realise that we are that machine.*

As we seek a greater understanding of ourselves and our potential, it is sensible to resist all attempts by mental trophy hunters to disturb our peace and make off with the secrets of our genius. Anyone interfering with the natural process of putrefaction that occurs when an author creatively decomposes their life story beneath the earth should be treated as the perpetrator of an abominable crime; and even those who endeavour to use blunt instruments of words to collapse our wave function into a soul-crushing Flatland should be driven away by maledictions equally baleful as the one adorning the grave of William Shakespeare.

In response to the fact that the virtual disinterment of the deceased writer raised more questions than it answered, the Reverend Patrick Taylor of Holy Trinity Stratford gave the wisest counsel when he said: "We shall have to live with the mystery of not knowing fully what lies beneath the stone."

The key thing here is that we *live* with not knowing, enduring with perpetual motion in the enigma of life instead of sacrificing every possibility to end it all for the temporary knowledge of a solitary death.

If we make ourselves sufficiently strong and silent we will be capable of containing The Secret, much like the skull of a mastermind that houses a vast library, or the tomb of an underground star that acts as a womb for their rebirth. By fortifying ourselves in this way, we paradoxically unseal our mysterious centre, the universal axis on which the wheel of fortune spins, so when the superposition of all possibilities, bounded in a nutshell, rolls into that black hole, we vanquish the beast of human error and are counted kings of infinite number.

So what *is* The Secret?

The dead Author-God's tombstone tells you all you need to know:

Cursed be the man who seeks to solve the mystery,
but blessed be he who becomes it.

'Domino!'

With the sense of a new perspective being opened up, I closed the book and, with a toss, returned it to the Library of Bedlam that existed all around me. Not only was the random selection of text eerily relevant to me, as it seemingly answered the question I posed before reading it, but the physical reality of the whole volume seemed to make a disclosure of its own by landing on its side and warping suggestively.

The peculiar manner in which the book fell, combined with the way the front cover bent backwards to meet its counterpart, seemed to allude to a time flip of some sort, perhaps even to the potential rediscovery of a youth before my youth, an impossible artefact with the power to put all the incongruous objects from my life decisively in their place.

Could it be the buckarastano the learned professor said I would come into contact with?

Before I could reach a definitive conclusion, the sound of my housekeeper opening the door and muttering something about an earthquake made me stand up and hurriedly brush the dust off my tweed jacket.

'Great grandchildren!' she screamed as she entered the room. 'You're . . . it's . . . I'm . . .'

'What's wrong, Susan? You look like you've seen a ghost.'

'I almost have! Look at yourself in the glass, professor!'

I turned to inspect my image in the mirror to which my housekeeper pointed and was shocked to see an older version of myself, with completely white hair and deep wrinkles, staring back at me. My mind must have been fractured like the window-pane because my first thought, following a moment of speech-less reflection on my speechless reflection, was that the figure staring out from the looking-glass world had no reason to be so upset since he was seeing a much younger form of himself in me. The two halves of the full picture, carrying more thoughts and memories than my poor head could hold, then came crashing together with deadly fire and motion in the place of the skull, like a bilateral terror attack carried out against me by the forces of reality.

'Odd's bodkin!' I cried. 'I've aged 30 years! I've gone from raven-haired to waving the white feather in a matter of hours! Oh, how my gorge rises at it! Never drink INK, Susan. Never con-sume it in any form. Don't ingest it or inject it, don't dry it and smoke it, don't inhale it or insufflate it. It's not worth the desic-cation. Look at me—I'm practically mummified! I extracted the meaning of my life story, and the paper it was written on has shrunk like the wild ass's skin! I've gone from flying in the face of Time to having monstrous crow's feet added to my lineaments in the blink of an eye. I've become a poor man's version of my-self, Susan. I'm Saint Faul the Apostle, Dorian Gray, Billy Shears and King Lear all rolled into a single third-class relic—and how abhorred in my imagination it is!'

'What can I do to help?' my housekeeper asked in a shaky voice. 'Should I call a doctor? Or the police? I've never heard of such a thing happening, not in all—'

'Wait!' I interrupted. 'I'm only focusing on the surface. What a dickey-dido I am to be lost so poorly in my superficies! How could I forget this new dimension the INK revealed to me, this new perspective, which is both mine and not mine? All is not lost, Susan! In fact, everything is to be gained! Oh, frabjous day! I can still rescue the story, so let's get to work on the double! All I need is a book, some glue and a little Casimir energy . . .'

HAMLET AND HIS DOUBLE (I)

Over the years, the issue of Hamlet's true age has generated a great deal of debate as well as a number of conflicting theories, and despite the play itself being more than four centuries old, the dispute over the lifespan of its protagonist is still as fresh as ever.

The reason for this lack of understanding is the limited perspective from which the problem is viewed, which causes us to regard the play as a two-dimensional object.

2D or not 2D? *That is the question.*

When we first join the action, everything about the Prince of Denmark is suggestive of youthfulness. From the lively manner in which he interacts with his school friend Horatio to the description of him by Laertes as "a violet in the youth of primy nature," the image we are presented with is unmistakably that of a young man, albeit one with the weight of the world on his shoulders.

Additionally, we learn that Hamlet has cut his schooling short by returning prematurely from the University of Wittenberg, suggesting he is still a teenager; and it only makes sense that the fatherless prince is not crowned king himself upon arriving back at the royal palace if he is considered too young to assume the responsibility of such a role.

By the time the fifth act is upon us, however, a major change has occurred, almost as if our tragic hero has suffered a time slip of some sort. When we witness the famous scene in which Hamlet handles the remains of Yorick and reflects on mortality, causing the two ravens of Thought and Memory to collide in the place of the skull, the Prince of Denmark seems to have aged suddenly because, as one of the other characters confirms, he is now *30 years old* . . .

The First Gravedigger, when asked how long he has been in his profession, says: "I have been sexton here, man and boy, thirty years," adding that he began "the very day that young Hamlet was born," which provides definitive confirmation of the prince's advanced age, a fact that is as hard to deny as it is to accept.

The key to understanding this apparent contradiction is hinted at by the fact that the jaw-dropping information is delivered by someone with a double, i.e. the First Gravedigger, who is paired with the Second Gravedigger, forming a matching set of sextons, like Tweedledum and Tweedledee with spades.

This scene exists apart from the rest of the drama in *Hamlet*, a step outside of the main action and therefore one step closer to the world inhabited by the audience; something which is even acknowledged by the First Gravedigger when he says to his familiar other "go, get thee to Yaughan, fetch me a stoup of liquor," referencing a real-life innkeeper who worked close to the Globe Theatre when the play was first performed. There is also a meta-joke made about everyone in England being as mad as Hamlet, which makes it clear to the audience that the grave scene has one foot in the world of fiction and one foot beyond it.

It is this play-outside-the-play that gives us the broadest view of the action, revealing a previously hidden dimension with which to make sense of the tragedy's inconsistencies. It is a heady perspective akin to an Author-God's-eye view, from which many wondrous things can be observed, including the character of Second Hamlet, who is much older and wiser than First Hamlet and whose intention to kill Claudius is much stronger.

Henry Mackenzie, in a periodical appropriately named *The Mirror*, referred to Hamlet as "a sort of double person" because of all his seemingly contradictory character traits. Mackenzie wrote: "The melancholy man feels in himself (if I may be allowed the expression) a sort of double person; one which, covered with the darkness of its imagination, looks not forth into the world, nor takes any concern in vulgar objects or frivolous pursuits; another, which he lends, as it were, to ordinary men, which can accommodate itself to their tempers and manners, and indulge, without feeling any degradation from the indulgence, a smile with the cheerful, and a laugh with the giddy. The conversation of Hamlet with the Grave-digger seems to me to be perfectly accounted for under this supposition."

Suddenly, if we look back on *Hamlet* via *The Mirror*, we see doubles everywhere. We have, to name but a few, Young Hamlet, the Prince of Denmark, and Old Hamlet, the King of Denmark, who was murdered before the start of the play, as well as a double of that double in Young Hamlet, the student we are introduced to in Act I, and Old Hamlet the more mature character who appears in Act V. But the doubles are not only to be found on the lateral plane, or the two-dimensional surface of the play; they are also located on the vertical axis, on larger and smaller scales, so the main characters have miniature doubles of themselves in the play-within-the-play as well as subtly implied "Big Others" on even higher stages that exist above our level of perception.

With this in mind, we can see Hamlet's instructions to the First Player as just one link in an endless chain of correspondences stretching from the microcosm to the macrocosm, from the very first light-sensitive "I" formed on the surface of the Globe to the ultimate observer at the end of time, with above reflecting below and vice versa, thanks to an ongoing dialogue between the stars of every theatrical system.

The advice that Hamlet, played by the First Player of *Hamlet*, gives to the First Player of *The Mouse-trap* is therefore the same speech that the hero of the meta-show would have given to "our" Hamlet just before the curtain went up on this performance:

> Be not too tame neither, but let your own discretion be your tutor. Suit the action to the word, the word to the action, with this special observance that you o'erstep not the modesty of nature. For anything so overdone is from the purpose of playing, whose end, both at the first and now, was and is to hold, as 'twere, the mirror up to nature; to show virtue her own feature, scorn her own image, and the very age and body of the time his form and pressure. Now this overdone, or come tardy off, though it make the unskilful laugh, cannot but make the judicious grieve; the censure of the which one must in your allowance o'erweigh a whole theatre of others.

It is now possible to recognise ourselves amongst the audience in that "theatre of others", and to confront the true "purpose of playing" in the dark mirror held up to nature . . .

The First Player on our plane of reality acts for us in the sense of performing actions that we are meant to observe, but he does so in the same way that the Player King acts "for" King Claudius in *Hamlet*: that is, to catch the conscience, to stir up uncomfortable memories and force a hidden reality to show its face—which means he is ultimately acting for a much higher purpose, that of a Superior First Player whom we have blocked from our minds.

This is the memory that the hero above is trying to awaken in us, that before the curtain went up on this world of ours, there were many obscure scenes involving murderous duplicity and destructive ambition, and we are somehow complicit in them. If we stop identifying with the criminal oppressor on this level, if we open our eyes to the clues sent down to us from the star of the show on a higher octave, all the incongruities will make sense as aspects of another reality reflected in our murky looking glass.

If we know how to read the signs, we can build up a vivid picture of the inner-upper dimensions and begin preparing ourselves to play the lead role therein, as a tesseractor in a tesseract, a penteractor in a penteract and so on. From our new perspective, we can perceive the colour-changing raven as it flies through the walls and bellows for revenge, with its extradimensional meaning as clear as day.

Action is opposed to Thought, while Thought is opposed to Memory, which means that if we *remember the unthinkable,* we *act* our way out of the simulation for good.

It's understood there's something you can do that can't be done, something whole that's two in one. It's Shakespeare in Hamlet and Hamlet in Shakespeare, the Beatles in Abbey Road and Abbey Road in the Beatles. It's Sirius A and Sirius B, e-book, p-book, particle and wave. It's Hugin and Munin closer than you'd think and exactly as close as you think at the same time.

It's in your hands and all in your head. *It's easy.*

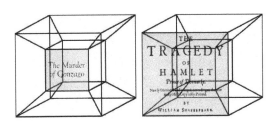

HAMLET AND HIS DOUBLE (II)

FIRST HAMLET:	*(Enter* FIRST HAMLET, *stage right.)*
	To be, or not to be . . .
SECOND HAMLET:	*(Enter SECOND HAMLET, jumping suddenly out of the shadows from stage left.)*
	That is the question!
FIRST HAMLET:	*(Shaking his head as if to assure himself that what he just heard was a figment of his imagination)* Whether 'tis nobler in the mind to suffer the slings and arrows of outrageous fortune . . .
SECOND HAMLET:	Or to take arms against a sea of troubles . . .
FIRST HAMLET:	And by opposing end them?
SECOND HAMLET:	To die.
FIRST HAMLET:	To sleep.
SECOND HAMLET:	No more.
FIRST HAMLET:	And by a sleep to say we end the heart-ache and the thousand natural shocks that flesh is heir to.
SECOND HAMLET:	'Tis a consummation devoutly to be wish'd.
FIRST HAMLET:	To die.
SECOND HAMLET:	To sleep.
FIRST HAMLET:	To sleep, perchance to dream.
SECOND HAMLET:	*(Walking over to* FIRST HAMLET *and speaking directly to him)* Ay, there's the rub; for in that sleep of death what dreams may come when we have shuffled off this mortal coil, must give us pause. *(He stops a short distance in front of* FIRST HAMLET *as he says the last word of the sentence.)*

FIRST HAMLET: There's the respect that makes calamity of so long life.

SECOND HAMLET: For who would bear the whips and scorns of time . . .

FIRST HAMLET: The oppressor's wrong . . .

SECOND HAMLET: The proud man's contumely . . .

FIRST HAMLET: The pangs of despised love . . .

SECOND HAMLET: The law's delay . . .

FIRST HAMLET: The insolence of office . . .

SECOND HAMLET: And the spurns that patient merit of the unworthy takes . . .

FIRST HAMLET: When he himself might his quietus make with a bare bodkin?

(He pulls out a glass cock and balls, partly filled with black ink, and points the object towards SECOND HAMLET, *as if threatening him with it.)*

SECOND HAMLET: *(Also pulls out a glass cock and balls and mirrors his counterpart's threatening pose.)*

Who would fardels bear, to grunt and sweat under a weary life . . .

FIRST HAMLET: *(Advances so he is chest-to-chest with* SECOND HAMLET, then *presses his cock against his counterpart's face and speaks through gritted teeth.)*

But that the dread of something after death . . .

SECOND HAMLET: *(Presses his cock against* FIRST HAMLET'S *face and speaks through gritted teeth.)*

The undiscover'd country from whose bourn no traveller returns . . .

FIRST HAMLET: (*Pushing his forehead against that of* SECOND HAMLET *like an aggressive stag*) Puzzles the will . . .

SECOND HAMLET: (*Pushing back with his forehead*) And makes us rather bear those ills we have than fly to others that we know not of?

FIRST HAMLET: (*Suddenly withdraws from his combative stance.*)
Thus conscience does make cowards of us all.

SECOND HAMLET: (*Takes a step back and suddenly seems forlorn.*)
And thus the native hue of resolution is sicklied o'er with the pale cast of thought.

FIRST HAMLET: And enterprises of great pith and moment with this regard their currents turn awry, and lose the name of action.

SECOND HAMLET: (*Hurriedly putting his cock back in its scabbard and motioning to* FIRST HAMLET *to do the same*)—Soft you now! The fair Ophelia!

FIRST HAMLET: (*Sheathing his cock*) Nymph, in thy orisons be all my sins remember'd.
(*Both* HAMLETS *disappear into the shadows as* OPHELIA *enters, dreamily singing 'All You Need is Death' by the Scarab Beatles. As she does so, the young woman picks out various flowers from a basket on her arm and discards them one by one on the floor. Eventually, she reaches the other side of the stage, where she opens a pair of curtains to reveal a large window, before which a crowd of angry people have gathered.*)

POLICEMAN:	(*Shouting up to* OPHELIA *at the palace window and struggling to make himself heard over the baying of the crowd behind him*) Good lady, the people call for an explanation of what they have seen. The masses cannot endure the enigma, they need an explanation to collapse the mystery into 2D.
OPHELIA:	Pray let's have no words of this; but when they ask you what it means, say you this: Belike this show imports the argument of the play.
POLICEMAN:	Which show?
OPHELIA:	Why, *The Mouse-escape*.
POLICEMAN:	Mean you *The Mouse-trap*?
OPHELIA:	From one perspective, yea.
POLICEMAN:	And which play?
OPHELIA:	Why, the *Uber-Hamlet*.
POLICEMAN:	But can you tell us its meaning?
OPHELIA:	That I cannot do.
	(*The rabble become so indignant at* OPHELIA's *refusal to provide a solution that they violently push past the* POLICEMAN *and begin shouting angrily at the impassive young woman at the window.*)
FIRST PERSON:	Speak, you posy-brained harlot, and put our ghost problem to bed! We came here to watch a play, not take part in one!

SECOND PERSON: Ay! Tell us what the dog is going on! We should be apart from the drama! We're audience members—we're above everything! Unlatch your lips and clear this mess up at once, you senseless mystery-monger!

OPHELIA: 'Tis a matter of communicating the living mystery to you, not of explaining it away. You'll just have to learn to—

FIRST PERSON: (*Interrupting*) Damn the balance of your house, you sweat-stewed she-herring! Tell us why there are doubles everywhere!

SECOND PERSON: And why am I so old?

OPHELIA: I can't tell you *exactly*, but—

FIRST PERSON: (*Interrupting again*) Then, you dim, dung-eyed hag, you fat, crooked-kidneyed caterpillar, you leave us with no choice!

SECOND PERSON: Prepare to have the meaning bashed out of you, you ill-faced, sodden-bosomed bug-breeder!

    (*The crowd climb through the window and begin smashing up everything on the stage. The* FIRST PERSON *and* SECOND PERSON *grab* OPHELIA *and drag her away to a nearby brook, in which she is forcibly drowned. As the poor maiden dies, the rest of the crowd continue with their campaign of vandalism until everything in sight has been completely destroyed.*)

THE END

THE TWIN TOWERS

In a secret underground laboratory, two forms of the Twin Paradox are created: one representing the famous physics thought experiment in print, the other in purely mental space. When the second version is brought down to the material world and published alongside its counterpart after 100 days in the head of a test subject, it becomes clear to the dark meaning researchers that the two accounts are now subtly different. Although the words are identical, their properties have been altered in a way that reveals a profound secret, one that Tweedledum had been keeping from Tweedledee, and Strength had been keeping from Mercy all these years.

In a secret underground laboratory, two forms of the Twin Paradox are created: one representing the famous physics thought experiment in print, the other in purely mental space. When the second version is brought down to the material world and published alongside its counterpart after 100 days in the head of a test subject, it becomes clear to the dark meaning researchers that the two accounts are now subtly different. Although the words are identical, their properties have been altered in a way that reveals a profound secret, one that Tweedledum had been keeping from Tweedledee, and Strength had been keeping from Mercy all these years.

This is how we constructed the Twin Paradox Towers. Building them up in a new dimension of meaning while also putting them down in writing for the comprehension of all Flatlanders proved to be both the easiest and the most difficult thing in the world, because such forms are designed to fall like dominoes and crash through the two-dimensional surface of the writing desk with the full force of polysemy.

This need not be a disaster, however, if North and South can find it within or between themselves to put their differences aside and realise they have more in common than they think— then even the seemingly unstoppable process of divine kwank can result in something other than tragedy.

'Although Hugin and Munin fly through the dome of the sky each day, I fear they won't return. I've received credible intelligence to suggest that the birds may be used in a terror attack against the inhabitants of Flatland, for love was let go of long ago, and the croaking raven doth bellow for revenge.'

However . . . the dome of the sky is also that of Odin's skull, and the mystery of Golgotha gives us a brand-new perspective akin to an Author-God's-eye view of the action, which is also a bird's-eye view of the spacious earth and heavens . . . so we see that Hugin and Munin *nevar* really went anywhere at all.

The same point reappears again and again, in different locations and different epochs, sometimes softly, sometimes fiercely, and seeing this from a new vantage point is what causes Mr Worm Hole to fall from the open beak of an astonished bird, down into the deepest shit on earth, the stinking black sludge in which the Tree of Meaning grows.

'Odd's bodkin!'

Strange all this difference should be

'twixt Sirius A and Sirius B.

2464 [hide] v t e
a secret:

all this difference
'twixt one and two
strange indeed it should be
but between me and you
and 'twixt you and me
all these differences
are *the same*

for there is but *one single difference*
in the whole universe

appearing at different times
and in different places
but always the selfsame dissimilarity

so to repeat:
there is *one difference only*
and it is *always the same*

DOMINOES

'man's search for meaning is symbolic'
he argued with a domino

'symbolic of what?'
his opponent countered

(the game was up)

this sign
this young man
whatshisface
frozen with fear
his nipples like dots
on a roman headstone

once the last tile is laid
the player must pick a spot
in the field
marked with a cross
a symbol of
whatchamacallit

the dominoes are symbols
but the symbols are dominoes
and when one is tipped
they all fall down

plays, sonnets
essays, stories
novels and biographies
all overturned
with a single movement

I follow the author's footnotes
to an unmarked grave
in a field left intentionally blank
the resting place is marked with a spot
also called a pip, a nip or dob
only god
his name
his initials
it turns out to be a blocking game
which moves me to declare
that I will not stand for this
by which I mean
I will not stand for something else

I will not be a what's-its-name
a doodah
a thingamabob
you understand

I will not fall for this
by which I mean
I will not fall for something else
in a lexical field in a foreign land

because it's obvious
that that which stands for me
in the act of falling
does not stand for me at all

I will not be
a signifier
a symbol
a domino

please don't let all this symbolise
what I think it symbolises
this is not a domino rally
this is not the author's intention

you count the pips
in the losing player's hand
separate the symbols from the signs
the men from the boys
and this can mean only one thing
your identity
was a phantom
that steered you through the world
and escorted you to this final resting spot

'domino!'

the heavier the weight of the tile
the more meaningful the symbol feels
the face

the word
the image
the name
the guinness world record for the longest wall of signs
set in stone and seen from outer space
but the first brick can refer to the last brick
so we are going round in circles
and if a symbol points to itself
then the whole structure is undermined

how do we explain it to aliens?
how do we explain
the rules of the game?

a player can change their old ideas
to incorporate new information
several interpretations can be made at once
but there are so many unreadable expressions
and no one can see the symbolic value
when the other players' faces are hidden

therefore I really must say
I will not fall for this
by which I mean
I will not fall for something else
I will not be a domino

I will not stand for this
I will not put up with sign after sign

I will not put up tile after tile
day after day
for you
or anyone else

I will not fall
for this game
of two-dimensional representation
in my name
by which I mean
I will not play the fall guy
for you
because
the ultimate truth tile
is blank

NOTES

'The Schrödinger's McCartney Experiment' was previously published by Queen Mob's Teahouse in 2016.

'A Warning to All Readers Regarding the Insidious Practice of Book Jamming' was previously published by Cricket Online Review in 2014.

'Seeing the Black Rectangle for What It Is' was previously published in 2014 as a pamphlet hidden inside the box of a black rectangle puzzle.

'The First Ever Human Being to Be Saved by the Loving Feather of Everything' was performed at St Pancras Hospital, London, on 23rd February 2018.

Stephen Moles is the author of several books, including the experimental and absurdist novels *All the World's a Simulation* and *The Most Wretched Thing Imaginable* (Sagging Meniscus Press) and *Paul Is Dead* (CCLaP), as well as numerous short stories and articles for the likes of Maudlin House, Nat. Brut, Spork and Disinformation. He is also the founder of the Dark Meaning Research Institute, a group of parasemantic investigators and kamikaze omniglots aiming to bring about the linguistic singularity for the benefit of humankind.

BLANK PAGE BOOKS

are dedicated to the memory of Royce M. Becker,
who designed Sagging Meniscus books from 2015–2020.

They are:

IVÁN ARGÜELLES
THE BLANK PAGE

JESI BENDER
KINDERKRANKENHAUS

MARVIN COHEN
BOOBOO ROI
THE HARD LIFE OF A STONE, AND OTHER THOUGHTS

GRAHAM GUEST
HENRY'S CHAPEL

JOSHUA KORNREICH
CAVANAUGH
SHAKES BEAR IN THE DARK

STEPHEN MOLES
YOUR DARK MEANING, MOUSE

M.J. NICHOLLS
CONDEMNED TO CYMRU

PAOLO PERGOLA
RESET

BARDSLEY ROSENBRIDGE
SORRY, I BROKE YOUR PROMISE

CHRISTOPHER CARTER SANDERSON
THE SUPPORT VERSES

Lightning Source UK Ltd.
Milton Keynes UK
UKHW011245221021
392644UK00003B/66